THE KINGFISHER TREASURY OF

Stories for
Seven
Year Olds

KINGFISHER
a Houghton Mifflin Company imprint
222 Berkeley Street
Boston, Massachusetts 02116
www.houghtonmifflinbooks.com

First published in 1992
2 4 6 8 10 9 7 5 3 1
1TR/0204/THOM/MA/115IWF(F)

LIBRARY OF CONGRESS CATALOGING–IN–PUBLICATION DATA
A treasury of stories for seven year olds/chosen by Edward & Nancy
Blishen: illustrated by Patricia Ludlow.—1st American ed.
p. cm.
"A read-aloud book"—Cover.
Summary: A collection of traditional and modern tales by such
authors as Rudyard Kipling, Arthur Ransome, and Charles Perrault.
1. Children's stories. 2. Tales. [1. Short stories.
2. Folklore.] I. Blishen, Edward. 1920–. II. Blishen, Nancy.
III. Ludlow, Patrica, ill. IV. Title: Treasury of stories for 7 year olds.
PZ5.T7654 1992
[E]–dc20   92-53109   CIP   AC

ISBN 0-7534-5713-X

Printed in India

THE KINGFISHER TREASURY OF

Stories for Seven Year Olds

CHOSEN BY EDWARD
& NANCY BLISHEN

ILLUSTRATED BY PATRICIA LUDLOW

KINGFISHER

BOSTON

CONTENTS

LION AT SCHOOL

Philippa Pearce

Once upon a time, there was a little girl who didn't like going to school. She always set off late. Then she had to hurry, but she never hurried fast enough.

One morning, she was hurrying along as usual when she turned a corner and there stood a lion, blocking her way. He stood waiting for her. He stared at her with his yellow eyes. He growled, and when he growled, the little girl could see that his teeth were as sharp as skewers and knives. He growled: "I'm going to eat you up."

"Oh, dear!" said the little girl, and she began to cry.

"Wait!" said the lion. "I haven't finished. I'm going to eat you up UNLESS you take me to school with you."

"Oh, dear!" said the little girl. "I couldn't do that. My teacher says we mustn't bring pets to school."

"I'm not a pet," said the lion. He growled again, and she saw that his tail swished from side to side in anger – *swish! swash!* "You can tell your teacher that I'm a friend who is coming to school with you," he said. "Now shall we go?"

The little girl had stopped crying. She said: "All right. But you must promise two things. First of all, you mustn't eat anyone: it's not allowed."

"I suppose I can growl?" said the lion.

"I suppose you can," said the little girl.

9

"And I suppose I can roar?"

"Must you?" said the little girl.

"Yes," said the lion.

"Then I suppose you can," said the little girl.

"And what's the second thing?" asked the lion.

"You must let me ride on your back to school."

"Very well," said the lion.

He crouched down on the sidewalk and the little girl climbed on his back. She held on by his mane. Then they went on together toward the school, the little girl riding the lion.

The lion ran with the little girl on his back to school. Even so, they were late. The little girl and the lion went into the classroom just as the teacher was calling the roll.

The teacher stopped calling the roll when she saw the little girl and the lion. She stared at the lion, and all the

other children stared at the lion, wondering what the teacher was going to say. The teacher said to the little girl: "You know you are not allowed to bring pets to school."

The lion began to swish his tail – *swish! swash!* The little girl said: "This is not a pet. This is my friend who is coming to school with me."

The teacher still stared at the lion, but she said to the little girl: "What is his name, then?"

"Noil," said the little girl. "His name is Noil. Just Noil." She knew it would not be a good idea to tell the teacher that her friend was a lion, so she had turned his name backward: LION – NOIL.

The teacher wrote the name down in her rollbook: NOIL. Then she finished calling the roll.

"Betty Small," she said.

"Yes," said the little girl.

"Noil," said the teacher.

"Yes," said the lion. He mumbled, opening his mouth as little as possible, so that the teacher should not see his teeth as sharp as skewers and knives.

All that morning, the lion sat up in his chair next to the little girl, like a big cat, with his tail curled around his front paws, as good as gold. He didn't speak unless the teacher spoke to him. He didn't growl; he didn't roar.

At recess, the little girl and the lion went into the playground. All the children stopped playing to stare at the lion. Then they went on playing again. The little girl stood in a corner of the playground, with the lion beside her.

"Why don't we play like the others?" the lion asked.

The little girl said, "I don't like playing because some of the big boys are so big and rough. They knock you over without meaning to."

The lion growled. "They wouldn't knock ME over," he said.

"There's one big boy – the very biggest," said the little girl. "His name is Jack Tall. He knocks me over on purpose."

"Which is he?" said the lion. "Point him out to me."

The little girl pointed out Jack Tall to the lion.

"Ah!" said the lion. "So that's Jack Tall."

Just then the bell rang again, and all the children went back to their classrooms. The lion went with the little girl and sat beside her.

Then the children drew and wrote until lunchtime. The lion was hungry, so he wanted to draw a picture of his dinner.

"What will it be for lunch?" he asked the little girl. "I hope it's meat."

"No," said the little girl. "It will be fish sticks, because today is Friday."

Then the little girl showed the lion how to hold the yellow crayon in his paw and draw fish sticks. Underneath his picture she wrote: "I like meat better than fish sticks."

Then it was lunchtime. The lion sat up on his chair at the dinner table next to the little girl.

The lion ate very fast, and at the end he said: "I'm still hungry; and I wish it had been meat."

After lunch, all the children went into the playground.

All the big boys were running around, and the very biggest boy, Jack Tall, came running toward the little girl. He was running in circles, closer and closer to the little girl.

"Go away," said the lion. "You might knock my friend over. Go away."

"Shan't," said Jack Tall. The little girl got behind the lion.

Jack Tall was running closer and closer and closer.

The lion growled. Then Jack Tall saw the lion's teeth as sharp as skewers and knives. He stopped running. He stood still. He stared.

The lion opened his mouth wide – so wide that Jack Tall could see his throat, opened wide and deep and dark like a tunnel to go into. Jack Tall went pale.

Then the lion roared.

He roared and he ROARED and he ROARED.

All the teachers came running out.

All the children stopped playing and stuck their fingers in their ears. And the biggest boy, Jack Tall, turned around and ran and ran and ran. He never stopped running until he got home to his mother.

The little girl came out from behind the lion. "Well," she said, "I don't think much of *him*. I shall never be scared of *him* again."

"I was hungry," said the lion, "I could easily have eaten him. Only I'd promised you."

"And his mother wouldn't have liked it," said the little girl. "Time for afternoon school now."

"I'm not staying for afternoon school," said the lion.

"See you on Monday then," said the little girl. But the lion did not answer. He just walked off.

On Monday, the lion did not come to school. At recess, in the playground, the biggest boy came up to the little girl.

"Where's your friend that talks so loudly?" he said.

"He's not here today," said the little girl.

"Might he come another day?" asked the biggest boy.

"He might," said the little girl. "He easily might. So you just watch out, Jack Tall."

HARE THE HERO

A Russian fairy tale

O nce upon a time, there was a little hare who was afraid of everything. He spent most of his time trembling. The sound of the wind, even a leaf falling, could make him jump. And being a hare, of course, when he jumped, he *jumped!* He was laughed at by all the other hares in the forest. *They* were afraid of the wolf, and the fox, and the bear, as any sensible animal would be. But they weren't afraid of the snow falling, or a bird suddenly taking off from the branch of a tree, as he was.

They called him Trembler.

And then one day, the little hare said to himself, "Now look here, you're not a little hare any longer! In fact, you're a big hare! *In fact*, you're one of the biggest hares in the forest. IN FACT, it's time you stopped trembling!" Another hare who happened to be going by asked, "Why are you talking to yourself, Trembler?"

"Don't you call me Trembler!" said the little hare who'd become a big hare. "I'm tired of being frightened! I'm not going to be frightened any more, by anything! I've done with trembling!"

And he went through the forest telling all the hares the same story. He had simply decided to be brave, that was it! Indeed, he meant to be *very* brave! "But what about the bear?" they asked. "The bear! I wouldn't give a couple of acorns for the bear!" "But what about the fox?" "The fox! I wouldn't give one of last year's beechnuts for the fox!" "But what about the wolf?" "The wolf had better look out, that's all I can say!" And the hare beat the ground with his feet as if it had been a drum.

Now, by chance, a wolf was prowling very near at hand. To tell the truth, he was hoping to catch a hare or two. He could hardly believe his luck when he heard the sounds of a hare or three talking – a hare or four – perhaps a hare or five. They'd gathered to hear Trembler beating his feet on the ground and boasting about what he'd do if he caught sight of a wolf. "And you can stop calling me Trembler!" he was yelling. "In future I would like to be called . . . Hare the Hero! When I've eaten up the first wolf to get in my way, I want everyone to call me HARE THE HERO!"

"Ho, ho!" thought the wolf. "So he's going to eat me up, is he? I wonder how he's going to do that? Well, if he manages it, they can call me Wolf the Weakling!" And he crept closer and got ready to spring.

At which moment Hare the Hero caught sight of him and was *terrified!* He wasn't just frightened; he was horribly scared! He didn't just tremble: he shook from head to foot. And without thinking, he leaped high into the air and came down on the wolf's back. He rolled down it, gave another tremendous leap, and took off as fast as he could – actually, even faster than that. He imagined he could feel

the wolf's hot breath on his tail. And surely that was the sound of the wolf's teeth snapping together, no more than an inch behind him! He ran until he could run no more. He ran until all the green trees in the forest became one huge, hot, green blur. Then he fell exhausted under the biggest and thickest bush he could see.

But where was the wolf?

Well, the wolf was running twice as fast in the other direction. When the hare gave his great leap and fell onto the wolf's back, he thought it was a gun being fired. A hunter! It must be a hunter! And while the hare was fleeing one way through the forest, believing the wolf's teeth were snapping together an inch behind his tail, the wolf was fleeing through the forest the other way, believing he could hear only an inch behind *his* tail the bang, bang, bang of shots from the hunter's gun.

It was a long time before the wolf slowed up, and a very long time before he thought it safe to stop running.

As for all the other hares, who'd dived into the nearest bushes, they took longer still to show their noses. And when they did, they talked about nothing but Trembler's bravery. Well, no – it certainly wasn't right to call him Trembler, any more. Hare the Hero, that was his name! "Did you see how he scared the life out of the wolf!" they asked one another. "He went for him without thinking twice about it!" And some said they'd seen Hare the Hero's teeth closing on the wolf's tail.

But where *was* Hare the Hero? Had he pursued the wolf? Might he even now be making a meal of him? They went searching through the forest. And at last they found him, lying panting under the biggest and thickest bush of all.

"Hare the Hero!" they cried. "Oh, there you are, Hare the Hero! And we thought you were boasting! Oh, Hare the Hero, how brave you are!"

"Brave?" said the hare. He stopped trembling and came out from under the bush. "Brave? Oh – why, yes, of course. You're right! I *am* brave!" And he beat with his feet on the ground as if it had been a drum. "And you're all . . . tremblers!" he cried.

And from that time on, even he believed that he was the bravest hare alive.

THE ROOSTER, THE CAT, AND THE SCYTHE

James Reeves

Old Matthew was a countryman living with his three sons in a cottage at the edge of a farm. He was very ancient and infirm. His eyes were dim, his voice weak, and his legs so feeble that before long he took to his bed. He had had a good life, though he had never saved any money. He was content to die, and only wished he had something to leave to his three sons, Peter, John, and Colin.

When he knew that his time had come, he called the three boys to his bedside and said in a quavering voice, "I must soon leave you, my sons, and I am sorry I have not much to give you. But what I have is yours. Peter, you shall have this fine rooster with his tall, red comb and his feathers of green and gold."

"You, John," went on the old man, "shall have my cat. He is not much to look at, but he is a good mouser. No place where he stays shall ever be troubled with mice."

John thanked the old man and took the cat. Then Matthew went on in his feeble voice, "As for you, Colin, I have nothing to give you but my scythe. With it I have cut grain and mowed grass for many years.' It is a good scythe.

Take it, and may you have good luck. These things are not much, but take them to lands where they are not known, and you shall learn their true value."

Then Matthew closed his eyes and fell asleep.

After the old man's death, Peter took the rooster and set out. But everywhere he went, he found that people had plenty of roosters and would give him nothing for such a common bird. In the towns, he saw that the church spires had gold roosters upon them to tell which way the wind was blowing, and in the country every farmyard had at least one rooster to wake the people every morning.

But Peter never gave up hope, and one day he reached an island where there were no roosters, and where no such bird had ever been seen. He showed the people the bird and said, "Look at him! See his tall red comb and his feathers of green and gold."

"He is indeed splendid to look at," said the people, "but of what use is he?"

"He will wake you every morning at the same time," said Peter. "As it is, you never know when to get up. Some of you sleep so long that you waste the best part of the day. Besides, every night, at regular intervals, he crows three times. But if he crows during daylight, you shall know that there is to be a change in the weather. Believe me, there never was a more useful bird in the world."

"You are right," said the people, "but is he for sale? How much do you want for him?"

"I want a donkey laden with as much gold as it can carry."

"Done!" said the people, who had plenty of gold. "That is not much to pay for such a fine bird."

So they gave Peter what he asked for, and off he went with his donkey laden with gold. Two great baskets it carried, and when Peter got home, his brothers were delighted.

"I, too, will go and make my fortune," said John.

So off he went with the cat.

But everywhere he went the people had all the cats they needed – black cats, white cats, ginger cats, and tabbies. They only laughed at John and told him to take his cat away and find something more useful. So off he went, till at last he came to an island where there were no cats. As you can imagine, the houses were overrun with mice. The people had done all they could to get rid of them, but still they came in their hundreds and ate up the grain and the cheese and the bread in their homes. No sooner had John let his cat loose than it caught a mouse, and then another and another and another, till everyone saw what a useful creature it was.

"That's not such a bad animal," they said. "It's not much to look at, but we can do with an animal like that. How much do you want for him?"

"I will let you have him," said John, "for as much gold as a horse can carry on its back." They agreed that this was not much to pay for the cat, so they gladly gave John what he asked for. When John at last got home with his horse laden with gold, his brothers were overjoyed. It was now the turn of Colin to see what luck he would have. So one bright morning, he sharpened the scythe his father had left him and set off into the world.

But everywhere he went, he found that the men carried scythes over their shoulders and went out each morning to cut the hay and the wheat.

"Won't you buy my scythe?" he asked. "It is a good scythe and used to belong to my father."

"We can see that," said the men, "for it is a very old-fashioned scythe. We have better ones ourselves. Be off with you, and see if you can find somebody who has never seen a scythe."

Well, this was exactly what Colin did. One day, he reached an island where no scythe had ever been seen. Yet the fields were full of ripe wheat, and Colin waited to see how the people would harvest it. When the time came, he was amazed to see that they did not cut the wheat down, but shot it down with cannons! All the guns on the island were brought out and fired with tremendous noise and smoke. The farm animals were terrified; dogs barked, cats howled, and hens and geese were too frightened to lay. Nor was this a very good way of harvesting the wheat, for some of it was shot near the top and the grain destroyed; some of the cannons fired right over the fields, and some of the cannon-balls were so hot that they set fire to the field and burned the wheat to the ground.

This was Colin's chance. He shouldered his scythe, and without noise or fuss cut down all the wheat in one field before the people could get to it with the cannons. They were so pleased that they asked him how much he would take for his scythe.

"That's much better than guns," they said. "Such an invention is worth having."

Colin told them they could have his scythe for a handcart full of gold, and this they gladly gave him. So off he went, without his scythe, but with a handcart of gold, which he pushed in front of him. When his brothers saw him, they were full of gladness. They prepared a noble feast to celebrate his homecoming, and afterward they put all their money together and bought a big farm on which they worked in peace and friendship for many years. You can be sure of one thing – or rather, of three things. They bought themselves first a rooster, to wake them in the morning, and next a cat, to keep down the mice in their barns. When harvest-time came around, they and their men worked with scythes to cut the grain, and never, never tried shooting it down with cannons.

JOHNNY-CAKE

Joseph Jacobs

Once upon a time, there was an old man, and an old woman, and a little boy. One morning, the old woman made a Johnny-cake and put it in the oven to bake. "You watch the Johnny-cake while your father and I go out to work in the garden." So the old man and the old woman went out and began to hoe potatoes, and left the little boy to tend the oven. But he didn't watch it all the time, and all of a sudden he heard a noise, and he looked up and the oven door popped open, and out of the oven jumped Johnny-cake, and went rolling along end over end, toward the open door of the house. The little boy ran to shut the door, but Johnny-cake was too quick for him and rolled through the door, down the steps, and out into the road long before the little boy could catch him. The little boy ran after him as fast as he could clip it, crying out to his father and mother, who heard the uproar, and threw down their hoes and gave chase, too. But Johnny-cake outran all three a long way and was soon out of sight, while they had to sit down, all out of breath, on a bank to rest.

On went Johnny-cake, and by and by, he came to two well-diggers who looked up from their work and called out: "Where ye going, Johnny-cake?"

He said: "I've outrun an old man, and an old woman, and a little boy, and I can outrun you, too-o-o!"

"Ye can, can ye? We'll see about that?" said they; and they threw down their picks and ran after him, but couldn't catch up with him, and soon they had to sit down by the roadside to rest.

On ran Johnny-cake, and by and by, he came to two ditchdiggers who were digging a ditch. "Where ye going, Johnny-cake?" said they. He said: "I've outrun an old man, and an old woman, and a little boy, and two well-diggers, and I can outrun you, too-o-o!"

"Ye can, can ye? We'll see about that!" said they; and they threw down their spades and ran after him, too. But Johnny-cake soon outstripped them also, and seeing they could never catch him, they gave up the chase and sat down to rest.

On went Johnny-cake, and by and by, he came to a bear. The bear said: "Where are ye going, Johnny-cake?"

He said: "I've outrun an old man, and an old woman, and a little boy, and two well-diggers, and two ditch-diggers, and I can outrun you, too-o-o!"

"Ye can, can ye?" growled the bear. "We'll see about that!" and trotted as fast as his legs could carry him after Johnny-cake, who never stopped to look behind him. Before long, the bear was left so far behind that he saw he might as well give up the hunt first as last, so he stretched himself out by the roadside to rest.

On went Johnny-cake, and by and by, he came to a wolf. The wolf said: "Where ye going, Johnny-cake?"

He said: "I've outrun an old man, and an old woman, and a little boy, and two well-diggers, and two ditch-diggers, and a bear, and I can outrun you, too-o-o!"

"Ye can, can ye?" snarled the wolf. "We'll see about that!" And he set into a gallop after Johnny-cake, who went on and on so fast that the wolf, too, saw there was no hope of overtaking him, and he, too, lay down to rest.

On went Johnny-cake, and by and by, he came to a fox that lay quietly in a corner of the fence. The fox called out in a sharp voice, but without getting up: "Where ye going, Johnny-cake?"

He said: "I've outrun an old man, and an old woman,

and a little boy, and two well-diggers, and two ditchdiggers, a bear, and a wolf, and I can outrun you, too-o-o!"

The fox said: "I can't quite hear you, Johnny-cake; won't you come a little closer?" and he turned his head a little to one side.

Johnny-cake stopped his race for the first time, and went a little closer, and called out in a very loud voice: "*I've outrun an old man, and an old woman, and a little boy, and two well-diggers, and two ditchdiggers, and a bear, and a wolf, and I can outrun you, too-o-o.*"

"Can't quite hear you; won't you come a *little* closer?" said the fox in a feeble voice, as he stretched out his neck toward Johnny-cake, and put one paw behind his ear.

Johnny-cake came up close, and leaning toward the fox screamed out: "I'VE OUTRUN AN OLD MAN, AND AN OLD WOMAN, AND A LITTLE BOY, AND TWO WELL-DIGGERS, AND TWO DITCHDIGGERS, AND A BEAR, AND A WOLF, AND I CAN OUTRUN YOU, TOO-O-O!"

"You can, can you?" yelped the fox, and snapped up the Johnny-cake in his sharp teeth in the twinkling of an eye.

THE FAIRY SHIP

Alison Uttley

L ittle Tom was the son of a sailor. He lived in a small whitewashed cottage in Cornwall, in England, on the rocky cliffs looking over the sea. From his bedroom window, he could watch the great waves with their curling plumes of white foam and count the seagulls as they circled in the blue sky. The water went right away to the dim horizon, and sometimes Tom could see the smoke from ships like a dark flag in the distance. Then he ran to get his spyglass, to get a better view.

Tom's father was somewhere out on that great stretch of ocean, and all Tom's thoughts were there, following him, wishing for him to come home. Every day, he ran down the narrow path to the small rocky bay and sat there waiting for the ship to return. It was no use to tell him that a ship could not enter the tiny cove with its sharp needles or rocks and dangerous crags. Tom was certain that he would see his sailor father step out to the strip of sand if he kept watch. It seemed the proper way to come home.

December brought wild winds that swept the coast. Little Tom was kept indoors, for the gales would have blown him away like a gull's feather if he had gone to the rocky pathway. He was deeply disappointed that he couldn't keep watch in his favorite place. A letter had come, saying that his father was on his way home and any time he might arrive. Tom feared he wouldn't be there to see him, and he stood by the window for hours, watching the sky and the wild tossing sea.

"What shall I have for Christmas, Mother?" he asked one day. "Will Santa Claus remember to bring me something?"

"Perhaps he will, if our ship comes home in time," smiled his mother, and then she sighed and looked out at the wintry scene.

"Will he come in a sleigh with eight reindeer pulling it?" persisted Tom.

"Maybe he will," said his mother, but she wasn't thinking what she was saying. Tom knew at once, and he pulled her skirt.

"Mother! I don't think so, I don't think he will," said he.

"Will what, Tom? What are you talking about?"

"Santa Claus won't come in a sleigh, because there isn't any snow here. Besides, it is too rocky, and the reindeer would slip. I think he'll come in a ship, a grand ship with blue sails and a gold mast."

Little Tom took a deep breath, and his eyes shone.

"Don't you think so, Mother? Blue sails, or maybe red ones. Satin like our parlor cushion. My father will come back with him. He'll come in a ship full of presents, and Santa will give him some for me."

Tom's mother suddenly laughed aloud.

"Of course he will, little Tom. Santa Claus comes in a sleigh drawn by a team of reindeer to the children of towns and villages, but to the children of the sea he sails in a ship with all the presents tucked away in the hold."

She took her little son up in her arms and kissed him, but he struggled away and went back to the window.

"I'm going to be a sailor soon," he announced proudly. "Soon I shall be big enough, and then I shall go over the sea."

He looked out at the stormy sea where his father was sailing, every day coming nearer home, and on that wild water he saw only mist and spray, and the cruel waves dashing over the jagged splinters of rock.

Christmas morning came, and it was a day of surprising sunshine and calm. The seas must have known it was Christmas, and they kept peace and goodwill. They danced into the cove in sparkling waves, and fluttered their flags of white foam, and tossed their treasures of seaweed and shells on the narrow beach.

Tom awoke early and looked in his stocking on the bed-post. There was nothing in it at all! He wasn't surprised. Land children had their presents dropped down the chimney, but he, a sailor's son, had to wait for the ship. The stormy weather had kept the Christmas ship at sea, but now she was bound to come.

His mother's face was happy and excited, as if she had a secret. Her eyes shone with joy, and she seemed to dance around the room in excitement, but she said nothing.

Tom ate his breakfast quietly – a bantam egg and some honey for a special treat. Then he ran outside, to the gate, and down the slippery, grassy path which led to the sea.

"Where are you going, Tom?" called his mother. "You wait here, and you'll see something."

"No, Mother. I'm going to look for the ship, the little Christmas ship," he answered, and away he trotted, so his mother turned to the house and made her own preparations for the man she loved. The tide was out, and it was safe now the winds had dropped.

She looked through the window, and she could see the little boy sitting on a rock on the sand, staring away at the sea. His gold hair was blown back, his blue sweater was wrinkled around his stout little body. The gulls swooped around him as he tossed scraps of bread to feed them. Jackdaws came whirling from the cliffs, and a raven croaked hoarsely from its perch on a rocky peak.

The water was deep blue, like the sky, and purple shadows hovered over it, as the waves gently rocked the cormorants fishing there. The little boy leaned back in his sheltered spot, and the sound of the water made him drowsy. The sweet air lulled him, and his head began to droop.

Then he saw a sight so beautiful he had to rub his eyes to get the sleep out of them. The wintry sun made a pathway on the water, flickering with points of light on the crests of the waves, and down this golden lane came a tiny ship that seemed no larger than a toy. She moved swiftly through the water, making for the cove, and Tom cried out with joy and clapped his hands as she approached.

The wind filled the blue satin sails, and the sunbeams caught the mast of gold. On deck was a company of sailors dressed in white, and they were making music of some kind, for shrill squeaks and whistles and pipings came through the air. Tom leaned forward to watch them, and as the ship came nearer, he could see that the little sailors were playing flutes, tootling a hornpipe, then whistling a carol.

He stared very hard at their pointed faces, and little pink ears. They were not sailor-men at all, but a crew of white mice! There were four-and-twenty of them – yes, twenty-four white mice with gold rings around their snowy necks, and gold rings in their ears!

The little ship sailed into the cove, through the barriers of sharp rocks, and the white mice hurried backward and forward, hauling at the silken ropes, casting the gold anchor, crying with high voices as the ship came to port close to the rock where Tom sat waiting and watching.

Out came the Captain – and would you believe it? He was a Duck, with a cocked hat like John Paul Jones, and a blue jacket trimmed with gold braid. Tom knew at once he was Captain Duck because under his wing he carried a brass telescope, and by his side was a tiny sword.

He stepped boldly down the gangway and waddled to the eager little boy.

"Quack! Quack!" said the Captain, saluting Tom, and Tom of course stood up and saluted back.

"The ship's cargo is ready, Sir," said the Duck. "We have sailed across the sea to wish you a Merry Christmas. You will find everything in order, Sir. My men will bring the merchandise ashore, and here is the Bill of Lading."

The Duck held out a piece of seaweed, and Tom took it. "Thank you, Captain Duck," said he. "I'm not a very good reader yet, but I can count up to twenty-four."

"Quack! Quack!" cried the Duck, saluting again. "Quick! Quick!" he said, turning to the ship, and the four-and-twenty white mice scurried down to the cabin and dived into the hold.

Then up on deck they came, staggering under their burdens, dragging small bales of provisions, little oaken

casks, baskets, sacks, and hampers. They raced down the ship's ladders, and clambered over the sides, and swarmed down the gangplank. They brought their packages ashore and laid them on the smooth sand near Tom's feet.

There were almonds and raisins, bursting from silken sacks. There were sugarplums and candy pouring out of wicker baskets. There was a host of tiny toys, drums and marbles, tops and balls, pearly shells, and a flying kite, a singing bird, and a music box.

When the last toy had been safely carried from the ship, the white mice scampered back. They weighed anchor, singing "Yo-heave-ho!," and they ran up the rigging. The Captain cried "Quack! Quack!," and he stood on the ship's bridge. Before Tom could say "Thank you," the little golden ship began to sail away, with flags flying, and the blue satin sails tugging at the silken cords. The four-and-twenty white mice waved their sailor hats to Tom, and the Captain looked at him through his spyglass.

Away went the ship, swift as the wind, a glittering speck on the waves. Away she went toward the far horizon along that bright path that the sun makes when it shines on water.

Tom waited till he could see her no more, and then he stooped over his presents. He tasted the almonds and raisins, he sucked the candy, he beat the drum, and tinkled the music box and the iron triangle. He flew the kite, and tossed the balls in the air, and listened to the song of the singing bird. He was so busy playing that he did not hear soft footsteps behind him.

Suddenly, he was lifted up in a pair of strong arms and pressed against a thick blue coat, and two bright eyes were smiling at him.

"Well, Thomas, my son! Here I am! You didn't expect me, now did you? A Happy Christmas, Tom, boy. I crept down soft as a snail, and you never heard a twinkle of me, did you?"

"Oh, Father!" Tom flung his arms around his father's neck and kissed him many times. "Oh, Father. I knew you were coming. Look! They've been, they came just before you, in the ship "

"Who, Tom? Who's been? I caught you fast asleep. Come along home, and see what Santa Claus has brought you. He came along o' me, in my ship, you know. He gave me some presents for you."

"He's been here already, just now, in a little gold ship, Father," cried Tom, stammering with excitement. "He's just sailed away. He was a Duck, Captain Duck, and there were four-and-twenty white mice with him. He left me all these toys. Lots of toys and things."

Tom struggled to the ground, and pointed to the sand, but where the treasure of the fairy ship had been stored, there was only a heap of pretty shells and seaweed and striped pebbles.

"They're all gone," he cried, choking back a sob, but his father laughed and carried him off, piggyback, up the narrow footpath to the cottage.

"You've been dreaming, my son," said he. "Santa Claus came with me, and he's brought you a fine bunch of toys, and I've got them at home for you."

"Didn't dream," insisted Tom. "I saw them all."

On the table in the kitchen lay such a medley of presents that Tom opened his eyes wider than ever. There were almonds and raisins in little colored sacks, and a music box with a picture of a ship on its round lid. There was a drum with scarlet edges, and a book, and a pearly shell from a far island, and a kite of thin paper from China, and a lovebird in a cage. Best of all there was a little model of his father's ship, which his father had carved for Tom.

"Why, these are like the toys from the fairy ship," cried Tom. "Those were very little ones, like fairy toys, and these are big ones, real ones."

"Then it must have been a dream-ship," said his mother. "You must tell us all about it."

So little Tom told the tale of the ship with blue satin sails and gold mast, and he told of the four-and-twenty white mice with gold rings around their necks, and the Captain Duck, who said "Quack! Quack!" His father sat listening, as the words came tumbling from the excited little boy.

When Tom had finished, the sailor said, "I'll sing you a song of that fairy-ship, our Tom. Then you'll never forget what you saw."

He waited a moment, gazing into the great fire on the
hearth, and then he stood up and sang this song to his son
and to his wife.

> There was a ship a-sailing,
> A-sailing on the sea.
> And it was deeply laden,
> With pretty things for me.
>
> There were raisins in the cabin,
> And almonds in the hold,
> The sails were made of satin,
> And the mast it was of gold.
>
> The four-and-twenty sailors
> That stood between the decks
> Were four-and-twenty white mice
> With rings about their necks.

39

The Captain was a Duck, a Duck,
With a jacket on his back,
And when this fairy-ship set sail,
The Captain he said "Quack."

"Oh, sing it again," cried Tom, clapping his hands, and his father sang once more the song that later became a nursery rhyme.

It was such a lovely song that Tom hummed it all that happy Christmas Day, and it just fitted into the tune on his music box. He sang it to his children when they were little, long years later, and you can sing it too if you like!

THE TORTOISE, THE MONKEY, AND THE BANANA TREE

A *tale from the Philippines*

Once upon a time, a tortoise was sunbathing by a river. You might think a tortoise, with its thick shell, couldn't sunbathe. But you'd be wrong. The warmth comes up from the ground, and, of course, the tortoise sticks its head out, and as much of its neck as it can. It's soon very warm indeed.

Well, this tortoise was almost asleep when she noticed a tree being carried downstream. And no ordinary tree, either. It was a banana tree. She dived in, swam to the tree, and began pushing it toward the bank. But a banana tree is a very big tree; and though this was a fair-sized tortoise, she couldn't pull it up the bank. The tree still had its roots and leaves, and they were heavy with water.

So the tortoise did the sensible thing – she ran for help. That's to say, she ran as a tortoise runs: a fairly slow business. But not far along the road, she came across her neighbor, the monkey.

"I say! Come and look!" said the tortoise. "I've found a banana tree. Help me carry it to my house so I can plant it there!"

The monkey thought for a moment, as monkeys do, and then he said:

"Right you are! But only if you agree that we share the tree."

Of course, said the tortoise. So they went to the river and, working together, just about managed to tug the tree up the bank and then drag it to the tortoise's yard. And the tortoise said, "Right. Now we'll dig a hole and plant it."

But the monkey thought for a moment, as monkeys do, and said, "You agreed we should share the tree, and I'm against planting it."

The tortoise said, "Of course, we'll plant it. Then we'll wait till bananas grow on it, and we'll share them. What else could be done with it?"

"What else?" said the monkey. "Well, to begin with, we could divide it up at once: half for you, half for me. That's much better than hanging around waiting for bananas to grow on it."

The tortoise grumbled, but the monkey said he wouldn't agree to anything else, so the tree had to be sawn in two.

The monkey looked at the two halves and decided the top of the tree looked the nicer half – much greener, not those dirty roots! – so he said, "I'll have the top half!"

And he seized the top of the tree, dragged it away to his

backyard next door, and planted it there. The tortoise was left with the bottom half of the trunk and the roots. This she planted with great care, pressing the earth down all around and watering it with can after can of water. While she did this, the tortoise was thinking; because tortoises think, just as monkeys do – but sometimes it's a better sort of thinking. Anyway, a slow smile began to spread across the tortoise's small, leathery face. And then she prepared to wait.

In the monkey's yard next door, the green top part of the banana tree soon turned brown, and the leaves dried and fell off. The tree began to lean sadly to one side, and soon it was dead. But the bottom half of the tree, in the tortoise's yard, put forth new leaves, and then flowers, and then bananas. They call the clumps of bananas, because of the way they grow, hands. Well, this tree was crowded with hands of ripening fruit.

And the smile on the tortoise's leather face grew larger and larger, until –

Until she began to wonder how she was going to pick the bananas.

I'm sure you see the problem. Tortoises, as is well known, cannot climb trees. From the beginning of time to the present moment, no tortoise has ever climbed a tree. And I very much doubt if a tortoise ever will.

The tortoise thought and thought, and as she did so, her smile changed to a frown, and her frown to a glare. She thought again, trying to think better thoughts than her first thoughts; but there was no way out of it. She knew only one creature able to climb the tree and pick the fruit, and that was her neighbor, the monkey.

So she put on the best face she could and went to visit him.

"Well, I'll pick the fruit for you," said the monkey, "but –"

"But what?" asked the tortoise, nervously.

"But I'll want half the bananas for my trouble," said the monkey.

Well, as they say, beggars can't be choosers; so the tortoise had to agree. And grinning broadly, the monkey shinned up the tree and, reaching the top, calmly began to

eat the bananas. Not one did he throw down to the waiting tortoise. "Hi!" cried the tortoise. "Half for you – half for me! Remember? So every time you eat one, throw one down to me."

But the monkey only laughed – the sort of laugh you get from a monkey when its mouth is full of delicious ripe bananas. "No," he said. "No! These are very good bananas, by the way. You must have looked after them very well! – No! You cheated me when we divided the tree. You let me take the worthless half, though I'm sure you knew it wouldn't grow. So now I'm going to eat every single banana!" And it began to rain banana skins as the monkey tossed them down from his perch at the top of the tree.

If tortoises could turn purple with rage, that tortoise would have turned purple with rage. As it was, she did some thinking; and then she crawled off to the other end of the yard and gathered some blackthorn branches. These she scattered on the ground under the tree. Then she hid.

The monkey came to the end of his feast and, very much heavier than when he went up, leaped down from the tree. He landed right in the middle of the thorns. "Ow!" he cried. "Ouch! Ow!" And he leaped from foot to foot, and shrieked and screeched. The tortoise, watching from where she lay hidden, smiled, and then laughed, and, if a tortoise could have split her sides, she'd have split her sides.

Which was the worst thing she could have done. That's to say, to laugh. For the monkey now knew where she was hidden, and he ran there and while she was helpless with laughter, picked her up and turned her on her back. And, as you know, a tortoise on her back is a useless tortoise. A tortoise on her back doesn't know how to get onto her front again.

"And now to punish you!" cried the monkey. "I'm not sure what's bad enough for you. Shall I beat you with a stick? No, that would be too kind! Shall I put you in a mortar, as if you were grain, and pound you to pieces? No, that would be too gentle!" He was still picking thorns out of his toes, and growing angrier and angrier. "I think throwing you off the top of a very high mountain might be about right!"

But the tortoise had been doing some upside-down thinking, and she said, "Oh, dear, do whatever you like with me: beat me with a stick, pound me to pieces in a mortar, throw me from the top of the highest mountain in the land: I don't mind, as long as you don't throw me in the water! Oh please, *don't* throw me in the water!"

"Ho, ho!" cried the monkey. "So that's what you're most afraid of! Right! Into the water you shall go!"

And he picked up the tortoise, carried her to the river, and threw her in. Splash! To the monkey's great delight, the tortoise disappeared under the water. "That's the end of you," he cried.

But at that very moment, here came the tortoise's head, above the water; and she was smiling. Then, with quick little movements of her legs, off she swam. And to the frowning monkey, the smiling tortoise said, "Thank you, you extremely foolish creature! I'd have thought even you would have known that water is my second home!"

And within a minute or so, or not much longer, she was out of sight.

THE TALE OF THE SILVER SAUCER AND THE TRANSPARENT APPLE

Arthur Ransome

There was once an old peasant, and he must have had more brains under his hair than ever I had, for he was a merchant and used to take things every year to sell at the big fair of Nijni Novgorod. Well, I could never do that. I could never have been anything better than an old forester.

"Never mind, grandfather," said Maroosia.

God knows best, and He makes some merchants and some foresters, and some good and some bad, all in His own way. Anyhow, this one was a merchant, and he had three daughters. There were none of them so bad to look at, but one of them was as pretty as Maroosia. And she was the best of them, too. The others put all the hard work on her, while they did nothing but look at themselves in the mirror and complain of what they had to eat. They called the pretty one "Little Stupid," because she was so good and did all their work for them. Oh, they were real bad ones, those two. We wouldn't have them in here for a minute.

Well, the time came around for the merchant to pack up and go to the big fair. He called his daughters and said, "Little pigeons," just as I say to you. "Little pigeons," says he, "what would you like me to bring you from the fair?"

Says the eldest, "I'd like a necklace, but it must be a very rich one."

Says the second, "I want a new dress with gold hems."

But the youngest, the good one, Little Stupid, said nothing at all.

"Now, little one," says her father, "what is it you want? I must bring something for you, too."

Says the little one, "Could I have a silver saucer and a transparent apple? But never mind if there are none."

The old merchant says, "Long hair, short sense," just as I say to Maroosia; but he promised the little pretty one, who was so good that her sisters called her stupid, that if he could get her a silver saucer and a transparent apple she should have them.

Then they all kissed each other, and he cracked his whip, and off he went, with the little bells jingling on the horses' harness.

The three sisters waited till he came back. The two elder ones looked in the mirror and thought how fine they would look in the new necklace and the new dress; but the little pretty one took care of her old mother, and scrubbed and washed and dusted and swept and cooked, and every day the other two complained that the soup was burned or the bread not properly baked.

Then, one day, there was a jingling of bells and a clattering of horses' hoofs, and the old merchant came driving back from the fair.

The sisters ran out.

"Where is the necklace?" asked the first.

"You haven't forgotten the dress?" asked the second.

But the little one, Little Stupid, helped her old father take off his coat and asked him if he was tired.

"Well, little one," says the old merchant, "and don't you want your fairing, too? I went from one end of the market to the other before I could get what you wanted. I bought the silver saucer from an old hag, and the transparent apple from a peddler."

"Oh, thank you, father," says the little one.

"And what will you do with them?" says he.

"I shall spin the apple in the saucer," says the little pretty one, and at that the old merchant burst out laughing.

"They don't call you 'Little Stupid' for nothing," says he.

Well, they all had their fairings, and the two elder sisters, the bad ones, they ran off and put on the new dress and the new necklace, and came out and strutted about, preening themselves like herons, now on one leg and now on the other, to see how they looked. But Little Stupid, she just sat herself down beside the stove, and took the transparent apple and set it in the silver saucer, and she laughed softly to herself. And then she began spinning the apple in the saucer.

Round and round the apple spun in the saucer, faster and faster, till you couldn't see the apple at all, nothing but a mist like a little whirlpool in the silver saucer. And the little good one looked at it, and her eyes shone like yours.

Her sisters laughed at her.

"Spinning an apple in a saucer and staring at it, the little stupid," they said, as they strutted around the room, listening to the rustle of the new dress and fingering the bright round stones of the necklace.

But the little pretty one did not mind them. She sat in the corner watching the spinning apple. And as it spun, she talked to it.

"Spin, spin, apple in the silver saucer." This is what she said. "Spin so that I may see the world. Let me have a peep at the little father Tsar on his high throne. Let me see the rivers and the ships and the great towns far away."

And as she looked at the little glass whirlpool in the saucer, there was the Tsar, the little father – God preserve him! – sitting on his high throne. Ships sailed on the seas, their white sails swelling in the wind. There was Moscow with its white stone walls and painted churches. Why, there were the market at Nijni Novgorod, and the Arab merchants with their camels, and the Chinese with their blue trousers and bamboo staves. And then there was the

great river Volga, with men on the banks towing ships against the stream. Yes, and she saw a sturgeon asleep in a deep pool.

"Oh! oh! oh!" says the little pretty one, as she saw all these things.

And the bad ones, they saw how her eyes shone, and they came and looked over her shoulder, and saw how all the world was there, in the spinning apple and the silver saucer. And the old father came and looked over her shoulder, too, and he saw the market at Nijni Novgorod.

"Why, there is the inn where I put up the horses," says he. "You haven't done so badly after all, Little Stupid."

And the little pretty one, Little Stupid, went on staring into the glass whirlpool in the saucer, spinning the apple, and seeing all the world she had never seen before, floating there before her in the saucer, brighter than leaves in sunlight.

The bad ones, the elder sisters, were sick with envy.

"Little Stupid," says the first, "if you will give me your silver saucer and your transparent apple, I will give you my fine new necklace."

"Little Stupid," says the second, "I will give you my new dress with gold hems if you will give me your transparent apple and your silver saucer."

"Oh, I couldn't do that," says the Little Stupid, and she goes on spinning the apple in the saucer and seeing what was happening all over the world.

So the bad ones put their wicked heads together and thought of a plan. And they took their father's ax, and went into the deep forest and hid it under a bush.

The next day, they waited till afternoon, when work was done, and the little pretty one was spinning her apple in the saucer. They said –

"Come along, Little Stupid; we are all going to pick berries in the forest."

"Do you really want me to come, too?" says the little one. She would rather have played with her apple and saucer.

But they said, "Why, of course. You don't think we can carry all the berries ourselves!"

So the little one jumped up, and found the baskets, and went with them to the forest. But before she started, she

ran to her father, who was counting his money and was not too pleased to be interrupted, for figures go quickly out of your head when you have a lot of them to remember. She asked him to take care of the silver saucer and the transparent apple for fear she would lose them in the forest.

"Very well, little bird," says the old man, and he put the things in a box with a lock and key to it. He was a merchant, you know, and that sort are always careful about things, and go clattering about with a lot of keys at their belt. I've nothing to lock up, and never had, and perhaps it is just as well, for I could never be bothered with keys.

So the little one picks up all three baskets and runs off after the others, the bad ones, with black hearts under their necklaces and new dresses.

They went deep into the forest, picking berries, and the little one picked so fast that she soon had a basket full. She was picking and picking, and did not see what the bad ones were doing. They were fetching the ax.

The little one stood up to straighten her back, which ached after so much stooping, and she saw her two sisters standing in front of her, looking at her cruelly. Their

baskets lay on the ground quite empty. They had not picked a berry. The eldest had the ax in her hand.

The little one was frightened.

"What is it, sisters?" says she; "and why do you look at me with cruel eyes? And what is the ax for? You are not going to cut berries with an ax."

"No, Little Stupid," says the first, "we are not going to cut berries with the ax."

"No, Little Stupid," says the second; "the ax is here for something else."

The little one begged them not to frighten her.

Says the first, "Give me your transparent apple."

Says the second, "Give me your silver saucer."

"If you don't give them up at once, we shall kill you." That is what the bad ones said.

The poor little one begged them. "O, sisters, do not kill me! I haven't got the saucer or the apple with me at all."

"What a lie!" say the bad ones. "You never would leave it behind."

And one caught her by the hair, and the other swung the ax, and between them they killed the pretty little one, who was called Little Stupid because she was so good.

Then they looked for the saucer and the apple, and could not find them. But it was too late now. So they made a hole in the ground and buried the little one under a birch tree.

When the sun went down, the bad ones came home, and they wailed with false voices and rubbed their eyes to make the tears come. They made their eyes red, and their noses, too, and they did not look any prettier for that.

"What is the matter with you, little pigeons?" said the old merchant and his wife. I would not say "little pigeons" to such bad ones. Black-hearted crows, I would call them.

And they wail and lament aloud –

"We are miserable forever. Our poor little sister is lost. We looked for her everywhere. We heard the wolves howling. They must have eaten her."

The old mother and father cried like rivers in springtime, because they loved the little pretty one, who was called Little Stupid because she was so good.

But before their tears were dry, the bad ones began to ask for the silver saucer and the transparent apple.

"No, no," says the old man; "I shall keep them forever, in memory of my poor little daughter whom God has taken away."

So the bad ones did not gain by killing their little sister.

"That is one good thing," said Vanya.

"But is that all, grandfather?" said Maroosia.

"Wait a bit, little pigeons. Too much haste set his shoes on fire. You listen, and you will hear what happened," said old Peter. He took a pinch of snuff from a little wooden box, and then he went on with his tale.

Time did not stop with the death of the little girl. Winter came, and the snow with it. Everything was white, just as it is now. And the wolves came to the doors of the huts, even into the villages, and no one stirred farther than he needed. And then the snow melted, and the buds broke on the trees, and the birds began singing, and the sun shone warmer every day. The old people had almost forgotten the little pretty one who lay dead in the forest. The bad ones had not forgotten, because now they had to do the work, and they did not like that at all.

And then one day, some lambs strayed away into the forest, and a young shepherd went after them to bring them safely back to their mothers. And as he wandered this way and that through the forest, following their light tracks, he came to a little birch tree, bright with new leaves, waving over a little mound of earth. And there was a reed growing in the mound, and that, you know as well as I, is a strange thing, one reed all by itself under a birch tree in the forest. But it was no stranger than the flowers, for there were flowers around it, some red as the sun at dawn and others blue as the summer sky.

Well, the shepherd looks at the reed, and he looks at those flowers, and he thinks, "I've never seen anything like that before. I'll make a whistle-pipe of that reed, and keep it for a memory till I grow old."

So he did. He cut the reed, and sat himself down on the mound, and carved away at the reed with his knife, and got the pith out of it by pushing a twig through it, and beating it gently till the bark swelled, made holes in it, and there was his whistle-pipe. And then he put it to his lips to see what sort of music he could make on it. But that he never knew, for before his lips touched it, the whistle-pipe began

playing by itself and reciting in a girl's sweet voice. This is what it sang:

"Play, play, whistle-pipe. Bring happiness to my dear father and to my little mother. I was killed – yes, my life was taken from me in the deep forest for the sake of a silver saucer, for the sake of a transparent apple."

When he heard that, the shepherd went back quickly to the village to show it to the people. And all the way, the whistle-pipe went on playing and reciting, singing its little song. And everyone who heard it said, "What a strange song! But who is it who was killed?"

"I know nothing about it," says the shepherd, and he tells them about the mound and the reed and the flowers, and how he cut the reed and made the whistle-pipe, and how the whistle-pipe does its playing by itself.

And as he was going through the village, with all the people crowding about him, the old merchant, that one who was the father of the two bad ones and of the little pretty one, came along and listened with the rest. And when he heard the words about the silver saucer and the transparent apple, he snatched the whistle-pipe from the shepherd boy. And still it sang:

"Play, play, whistle-pipe! Bring happiness to my dear father and to my little mother. I was killed – yes, for my life was taken from me in the deep forest for the sake of a silver saucer, for the sake of a transparent apple."

And the old merchant remembered the little good one, and his tears trickled over his cheeks and down his old beard. Old men love little pigeons, you know. And he said to the shepherd –

"Take me at once to the mound, where you say you cut the reed."

The shepherd led the way, and the old man walked beside him, crying, while the whistle-pipe in his hand went on singing and reciting its little song over and over again.

They came to the mound under the birch tree, and there were the flowers, shining red and blue, and there in the middle of the mound was the stump of the reed which the shepherd had cut.

The whistle-pipe sang on and on.

Well, there and then, they dug up the mound, and there was the little girl lying under the dark earth as if she were fast asleep.

"O, God of mine," says the old merchant, "this is my daughter, my little pretty one, whom we called Little Stupid." He began to weep loudly and wring his hands; but the whistle-pipe, playing and reciting, changed its song. This is what it sang:

"My sisters took me into the forest to look for the red berries. In the deep forest, they killed poor me for the sake of a silver saucer, for the sake of a transparent apple. Wake me, dear father, from a bitter dream, by fetching water from the well of the Tsar."

How the people scowled at the two sisters! They scowled, they cursed them for the bad ones they were. And the bad ones, the two sisters, wept, and fell on their knees, and confessed everything. They were taken, and their hands were tied, and they were shut up in prison.

"Do not kill them," begged the old merchant, "for then I should have no daughters at all, and when there are no fish in the river, we make shift with crays. Besides, let me go to the Tsar and beg water from his well. Perhaps my little daughter will wake up, as the whistle-pipe tells us."

And the whistle-pipe sang again:

"Wake me, wake me, dear father, from a bitter dream, by fetching water from the well of the Tsar. Till then, dear father, a blanket of black earth and the shade of the green birch tree."

So they covered the little girl with her blanket of earth, and the shepherd with his dogs watched the mound night and day. He begged for the whistle-pipe to keep him company, poor lad, and all the days and nights he thought of the sweet face of the little pretty one he had seen there under the birch tree.

The old merchant harnessed his horse, as if he were going to the town; and he drove off through the forest, along the roads, till he came to the palace of the Tsar, the little father of all good Russians. And then he left his horse and cart and waited on the steps of the palace.

The Tsar, the little father, with rings on his fingers and a gold crown on his head, came out on the steps in the

morning sunshine; and as for the old merchant, he fell on his knees and kissed the feet of the Tsar, and begged –

"O little father, Tsar, give me leave to take water – just a little drop of water – from your holy well."

"And what will you do with it?" says the Tsar.

"I will wake my daughter from a bitter dream," says the old merchant. "She was murdered by her sisters – killed in the deep forest – for the sake of a silver saucer, for the sake of a transparent apple."

"A silver saucer?" says the Tsar – "a transparent apple? Tell me about that."

And the old merchant told the Tsar everything, just as I have told it to you.

And the Tsar, the little father, he gave the old merchant a glass of water from his holy well. "But," says he, "when your daughterkin wakes, bring her to me, and her sisters with her, and also the silver saucer and the transparent apple."

The old man kissed the ground before the Tsar, and took the glass of water and drove home with it, and I can tell you he was careful not to spill a drop. He carried it all the way in one hand as he drove.

He came to the forest and to the flowering mound under the little birch tree, and there was the shepherd watching with his dogs. The old merchant and the shepherd took away the blanket of black earth. Tenderly, the shepherd used his fingers, until the little girl, the pretty one, the good one, lay there as sweet as if she were not dead.

Then the merchant scattered the holy water from the glass over the little girl. And his daughterkin blushed as she lay there, and opened her eyes, and passed a hand across them, as if she were waking from a dream. And then she leaped up, crying and laughing, and clung around her old father's neck. And there they stood, the two of them, laughing and crying with joy. And the shepherd could not take his eyes from her, and in his eyes there were tears.

But the old father did not forget what he had promised the Tsar. He set the little pretty one, who had been so good that her wicked sisters had called her Stupid, to sit beside him on the cart. And he brought something from the house in a coffer of wood and kept it under his coat. And they

brought out the two sisters, the bad ones, from their dark prison and set them in the cart. And the Little Stupid kissed them and cried over them, and wanted to loose their hands, but the old merchant would not let her. And they all drove together till they came to the palace of the Tsar. The shepherd boy could not take his eyes from the little pretty one, and he ran all the way behind the cart.

Well, they came to the palace, and waited on the steps; and the Tsar came out to take the morning air, and he saw the old merchant, and the two sisters with their hands tied, and the little pretty one, as lovely as a spring day. And the Tsar saw her and could not take his eyes from her. He did not see the shepherd boy, who hid away among the crowd.

Says the great Tsar to his soldiers, pointing to the bad sisters, "These two are to be put to death at sunset. When the sun goes down, their heads must come off, for they are not fit to see another day."

Then he turns to the little pretty one, and he says: "Little sweet pigeon, where is your silver saucer, and where is your transparent apple?"

The old merchant took the wooden box from under his coat, and opened it with a key at his belt, and gave it to the little one, and she took out the silver saucer and the transparent apple and gave them to the Tsar.

"O lord Tsar," says she, "spin the apple in the saucer, and you will see whatever you wish to see – your soldiers, your high hills, your forests, your plains, your rivers, and everything in all Russia." And the Tsar, the little father, spun the apple in the saucer till it seemed a little whirlpool of white mist, and there he saw glittering towns, and regiments of soldiers marching to war, and ships, and day and night, and the clear stars above the trees. He looked at these things and thought much of them.

Then the little good one threw herself on her knees before him, weeping.

"O little father, Tsar," she says, "take my transparent apple and my silver saucer; only forgive my sisters. Do not kill them because of me. If their heads are cut off when the sun goes down, it would have been better for me to lie under the blanket of black earth in the shade of the birch tree in the forest."

The Tsar was pleased with the kind heart of the little pretty one, and he forgave the bad ones, and their hands were untied, and the little pretty one kissed them, and they kissed her again and said they were sorry.

The old merchant looked up at the sun, and saw how the time was going.

"Well, well," says he, "it's time we were getting ready to go home."

They all fell on their knees before the Tsar and thanked him. But the Tsar could not take his eyes from the little pretty one and would not let her go.

"Little sweet pigeon," says he, "will you be my Tsaritza, and a kind mother to Holy Russia?"

And the little good one did not know what to say. She blushed and answered, very rightly, "As my father orders, and as my little mother wishes, so shall it be."

The Tsar was pleased with her answer, and he sent a messenger on a galloping horse to ask leave from the little pretty one's old mother. And of course the old mother said that she was more than willing. So that was all right. Then there was a wedding – such a wedding! – and every city in Russia sent a silver plate of bread, and a golden salt-cellar, with their good wishes to the Tsar and Tsaritza.

Only the shepherd boy, when he heard that the little pretty one was to marry the Tsar, turned sadly away.

"Are you happy, little sweet pigeon?" says the Tsar.

"Oh, yes," says the Little Stupid, who was now Tsaritza and mother of Holy Russia; "but there is one thing that would make me happier."

"And what is that?" says the lord Tsar.

"I cannot bear to lose my old father and my little mother and my dear sisters. Let them be with me here in the palace, as they were in my father's house."

The Tsar laughed at the little pretty one, but he agreed, and the little pretty one ran to tell them the good news. She said to her sisters, "Let all be forgotten, and all be forgiven, and may the evil eye fall on the one who first speaks of what has been!"

For a long time the Tsar lived, and the little pretty one the Tsaritza, and they had many children and were very happy together. And ever since then, the Tsars of Russia have kept the silver saucer and the transparent apple, so that, whenever they wish, they can see everything that is going on all over Russia. Perhaps even now the Tsar, the little father – God preserve him! – is spinning the apple in the saucer, and looking at us, and thinking it is time that two little pigeons were in bed.

"Is that the end?" said Vanya.

"That is the end," said old Peter.

"Poor shepherd boy!" said Maroosia.

"I don't know about that," said old Peter. "You see, if he had married the little pretty one and had to have all the family to live with him, he would have had them in a hut like ours instead of in a great palace, and so he would never have had room to get away from them. And now, little pigeons, who is going to be first into bed?"

THE SING-SONG OF OLD MAN KANGAROO

Rudyard Kipling

Not always was the Kangaroo as now we do behold him, but a Different Animal with four short legs. He was gray and he was woolly, and his pride was inordinate: he danced on an outcrop in the middle of Australia, and he went to the Little God Nqa.

He went to Nqa at six before breakfast, saying, "Make me different from all other animals by five this afternoon."

Up jumped Nqa from his seat on the sand-flat and shouted, "Go away!"

He was gray and he was woolly, and his pride was inordinate: he danced on a rock ledge in the middle of Australia, and he went to the Middle God Nquing.

He went to Nquing at eight after breakfast, saying, "Make me different from all other animals; make me, also, wonderfully popular by five this afternoon."

Up jumped Nquing from his burrow in the spinifex and shouted, "Go away!"

He was gray and he was woolly, and his pride was inordinate: he danced on a sandbank in the middle of Australia, and he went to the Big God Nqong.

He went to Nqong at ten before dinnertime, saying, "Make me different from all other animals; make me popular and wonderfully run after by five this afternoon."

Up jumped Nqong from his bath in the salt-pan and shouted, "Yes, I will!"

Nqong called Dingo – Yellow-Dog Dingo – always hungry, dusty in the sunshine, and showed him Kangaroo. Nqong said, "Dingo! Wake up, Dingo! Do you see that gentleman dancing on an ashpit? He wants to be popular and very truly run after. Dingo, make him so!"

Up jumped Dingo – Yellow-Dog Dingo – and said, "What, *that* cat-rabbit?"

Off ran Dingo – Yellow-Dog Dingo – always hungry, grinning like a coal-scuttle – ran after Kangaroo.

Off went the proud Kangaroo on his four little legs like a bunny.

This, O Beloved of mine, ends the first part of the tale!

He ran through the desert; he ran through the mountains; he ran through the salt-pans; he ran through the reed-beds; he ran through the blue gums; he ran through the spinifex; he ran till his front legs ached.

He had to!

Still ran Dingo – Yellow-Dog Dingo – always hungry, grinning like a rat-trap, never getting nearer, never getting farther – ran after Kangaroo.

He had to!

Still ran Kangaroo – Old Man Kangaroo. He ran through the ti-trees; he ran through the mulga; he ran through the long grass; he ran through the short grass; he ran through the Tropics of Capricorn and Cancer; he ran till his hind legs ached.

He had to!

Still ran Dingo – Yellow-Dog Dingo – always hungry, grinning like a horse-collar, never getting nearer, never getting farther; and they came to the Wollgong River.

Now, there wasn't any bridge, and there wasn't any ferry-boat, and Kangaroo didn't know how to get over; so he stood on his legs and hopped.

He had to!

He hopped through the Flinders; he hopped through the Cinders; he hopped through the deserts in the middle of Australia. He hopped like a Kangaroo.

First he hopped one yard; then he hopped three yards; then he hopped five yards; his legs growing stronger; his legs growing longer. He hadn't any time for rest or refreshment, and he wanted them very much.

Still ran Dingo – Yellow-Dog Dingo – very much bewildered, very much hungry, and wondering what in the world or out of it made Old Man Kangaroo hop.

For he hopped like a cricket; like a pea in a saucepan; or a new rubber ball on a nursery floor.

He had to!

He tucked up his front legs; he hopped on his hind legs; he stuck out his tail for a balance-weight behind him; and he hopped through the Darling Downs.

He had to!

Still ran Dingo – Tired-Dog Dingo – hungrier and hungrier, very much bewildered, and wondering when in the world or out of it would Old Man Kangaroo stop.

Then came Nqong from his bath in the salt-pans, and said, "It's five o'clock."

Down sat Dingo – Poor-Dog Dingo – always hungry, dusty in the sunshine; hung out his tongue and howled.

Down sat Kangaroo – Old Man Kangaroo – stuck out his tail like a milking-stool behind him, and said, "Thank goodness *that's* finished!"

Then said Nqong, who is always a gentleman, "Why aren't you grateful to Yellow-Dog Dingo? Why don't you thank him for all he has done for you?"

Then said Kangaroo – Tired Old Kangaroo – "He's chased me from the homes of my childhood; he's chased me out of my regular mealtimes; he's altered my shape so I'll never get it back; and he's played Old Scratch with my legs."

Then said Nqong, "Perhaps I'm mistaken, but didn't you ask me to make you different from all other animals, and to make you very truly sought after? And now it is five o'clock."

"Yes," said Kangaroo. "I wish that I hadn't. I thought you would do it by charms and incantations, but this is a practical joke."

"Joke!" said Nqong, from his bath in the blue gums. "Say that again, and I'll call up Dingo to run your hind legs off."

"No," said the Kangaroo. "I must apologize. Legs are legs, and you needn't alter 'em so far as I am concerned. I only meant to explain to Your Lordliness that I've had nothing to eat since morning, and I'm very empty indeed."

"Yes," said Dingo – Yellow-Dog Dingo – "I am just in the same situation. I've made him different from all other animals; but what may I have for my tea?"

Then said Nqong from his bath in the salt-pan, "Come and ask me about it tomorrow, because I'm going to wash."

So they were left in the middle of Australia, Old Man Kangaroo and Yellow-Dog Dingo, and each said, "That's *your* fault."

CAT AND MOUSE

Margaret Mahy

One summer's day, a young mouse set out looking for adventure.

"Be very careful!" said his mother. "It's a dangerous world for mice. Watch out for traps, and watch out for the sharp claws of the cat, and, above all, don't be too sure of anything."

As the mouse ran in and out of the stems of the sunflowers, a cat saw him and called out in a sweet voice, "Hello there, Mouse!"

The mouse stopped, hearing his name called, and looked out nervously.

"Come on out, Mouse, and talk to me," the cat said. "I'm rather lonely, and I'd love a bit of company."

"But aren't you a cat?" asked the young and innocent mouse.

"A cat? Perish the thought!" cried the cat piously. "I am none other than Santa Claus. Look at my white whiskers and white eyebrows if you don't believe me."

"Are you absolutely *sure* you're Santa Claus?" he asked, because there was still something about the cat that made him very suspicious.

"Of course I am," said the cat. "Look! Here are my claws to prove it. That's why I'm called Santa Claus. Come on out. I have presents and things for you just down the path."

The mouse had heard that Santa Claus had white whiskers and white eyebrows, and also that he gave people presents.

As the mouse came out from among the sunflower stems, the cat pounced on him, catching him straight away.

"You should never believe everything you hear," the cat said, "because now I am going to eat you up."

"You said we'd talk together," cried the terrified mouse, realizing he had been tricked.

"Well, we'll talk a bit first if you like," said the cat. "And then I'll eat you up afterward. I have plenty of time, and I'm not terribly hungry. I just liked the thought of catching a mouse."

The mouse thought very quickly.

"What makes you so sure I am a mouse?" he asked. "You're not very clever for a cat."

"Well, you *are* a mouse," said the cat.

The mouse made himself laugh very hard. He didn't feel much like laughing. He just made himself laugh through sheer willpower.

"I'm not a mouse," he said, when he had finished laughing, "I'm a dog."

It was the cat's turn to laugh, but it was a very surprised laugh. He had never caught a mouse like this one before.

"I know a mouse when I see one."

"No – I'm definitely a dog!" declared the mouse, still

laughing, "and when I get my breath back, I'm going to bark at you and chase you up a tree."

Inside his mouse-mind he was telling himself: I'm not a mouse . . . I'm a dog. I'm *not* a mouse. I'm a *dog*. He made himself think dog thoughts.

"Just imagine you thinking that I am a mouse!" he cried.

"Well, you look *quite* like a mouse," the cat said, sounding rather less sure of himself. The mouse was looking a lot more like a dog than the cat had thought at first.

"Let me hear you bark!" the cat commanded.

"Wait a moment . . ." In his mouse-mind he was telling himself: Think *dog*! Bark *dog*! Be *dog*! "Well, are you ready?"

"Yes!" said the cat.

"Then stand back a bit because I don't want to deafen you with my barking," the mouse said, and the cat actually did stand back a bit, though he kept one paw firmly on the mouse's tail. The mouse barked as well as he could, but it came out very like a mouse's squeak.

"There!" said the cat triumphantly, "and I'm going to eat you straight away because I can see you're a very tricky mouse."

The mouse did not lose his head, even though he thought the cat might take it off with a single bite.

"You really do have mice on the brain. It'll serve you right when I chase you up a tree."

"Think *dog*! Be *dog*!" he muttered under his whiskers. He made himself laugh in an easygoing fashion.

As he spoke, a strange thing happened to the mouse. By now he believed he actually *was* a dog. The cat, which had looked so terrible a moment ago, began to look small and silly. Cowardly, too! He felt *dogness* swell up inside him. He thought he could remember burying bones, fighting other

dogs, and, of course, chasing many, many cats. He felt a bark swelling in his throat. He barked again.

My goodness! the cat thought. He really *is* a dog, and here I am with my paw on his tail. The cat looked nervous, and the mouse felt very strong. He opened his mouth and barked for the third time. This time, there was no doubt about it: it was a really wonderful bark. The cat took his paw off the mouse's tail and ran for the trees with the mouse chasing him, barking furiously. The cat shot up the tree like a furry rocket and hid among the leaves.

Whew! That was a narrow escape, thought the cat, cowering at the top of the tree.

Whew! That was a narrow escape, thought the mouse at the bottom of the tree. "I'm off home to Mother!"

As he reached the mousehole, he saw his mother, nervously collecting sunflower seeds outside.

"Mother!" called the mouse. "Here I am, home again."

"Ahhhhh! A dog!" screamed his mother and popped down into the mousehole.

The mouse lay outside in the sun with his paws stretched in front of him and his tongue hanging out.

"Think *mouse*," he panted. "Think *mouse*!"

So he thought *mouse*, and, as he thought *mouse*, the *dogness* died away.

"What am I doing sitting out here in broad daylight with my tongue hanging out?" he squeaked to himself. "I must be mad. That cat could come back at any moment."

Then he scuttled into the mousehole, where his mother met him with great delight.

"I'm glad you're back," she said. "It's dangerous out there. A big dog ran at me, barking."

"A cat caught me," the mouse said, "but I escaped."

"Escaped? Oh, my son! How did you manage that?"

"Cleverness," said the mouse modestly. "Cleverness and courage. I chased the cat up the tree."

Exaggerating again, thought his mother, fondly.

Then the mouse and his mother had a delicious dinner of sunflower seeds.

As for the cat, he stayed up in the tree all day for fear of the savage dog that was waiting somewhere below in the summer garden.

BEAUTIFUL CATHARINELLA

The Brothers Grimm

Long long ago, in a village in Italy, lived a man and his wife who had a daughter called Catharinella. She had such lovely fair hair that words cannot describe how beautiful were the braids wound around her head.

The father was a soldier, and just when a new baby was to be born, he was called away to the wars. At that time, the mother was always hungry for parsley and soon had eaten up all there was in her garden. Next she went the round of her neighbors' gardens, till at length there wasn't the tiniest sprig of parsley left in the whole village. The only bit remaining near grew in the garden of an ogre who lived in a great palace outside the village.

The poor woman wept and was very unhappy, because she feared that she and her unborn child would die of starvation. Seeing the sad state her dear mother was in, Catharinella too was sad, and at last she decided to go every day and steal as much parsley from the ogre's garden as her mother wanted. When the ogre went around each evening to see how his garden grew, he found the parsley plants getting fewer and fewer; and he shook his head angrily, while his long beard swept the box-hedge lining the beds on both sides. As this did not seem to mend matters much, he at last strewed ashes secretly along the path.

So, in the morning when Catharinella went as usual to fetch her mother's parsley, the ashes stuck to her little slippers, and the ogre easily traced the way to her cottage. He followed her in and, appearing to be very angry, he threatened that unless she came to the palace as his servant he would eat her. The poor mother sobbed bitterly, not wanting the girl to go; but when the ogre promised that no harm would come to her – he would even let her pick each day all the parsley her mother wanted – it was agreed, and Catharinella departed with her new master.

Now the ogre was not really as fierce and wicked as he looked, but just a little lazy; and when he came home in the evening after eating heartily, he hated to climb the stairs. So he shouted from below the window, "Catharinella, Catharinella, let your golden braids down and lift me into the house," and the girl did so; and that was all the work she had to do. She enjoyed an easy life, with plenty to eat and drink; and she had lots of fun talking to the furniture, for it was enchanted.

As he got older, the ogre grew lazier and lazier, till he didn't want to do a thing for himself, and even took in a young man to help with the magic. This was a smart, nice-looking fellow, who had not got a long beard, nor did he wait long at the door when *he* wished to see Catharinella – no, he leaped up the stairs, drawn by the beautiful golden braids in quite a different way from the ogre! Every day, the ogre seemed heavier and heavier to the girl, and she disliked him so much that she was well pleased when the young wizard offered to conjure up a coach and horses to take them away.

Soon everything was ready for their flight, but as all the pieces of furniture could talk, the pair were afraid they might blab and the old ogre would learn where they had gone – and before they were far enough off for him not to catch up with them. So they thought and they thought what they could do to keep the furniture quiet. At last, Catharinella decided she would cook a great potful of macaroni and treat them, lock, stock, and barrel, to this tasty dish. She soon set to work, and when the macaroni was cooked, she stood the great pot in the main hall and invited everything in the house to eat its fill. It must have been a funny sight indeed to see chairs, settles, tables, and all, come running! – mirrors and pictures flying down off the walls; stout old cupboards stumbling along; china sets and glasses tripping lightly – all to enjoy the treat. They made a dreadful din, all the big and little mouths busily munching, and even the great pot itself now and again gulping down some of its own contents. When they had eaten all they could, they promised to say nothing that would betray the kind folk who had fed them. And in fact, all would have been well, if an old broom in a corner of the attic had not been forgotten. He went stumping around the house in a rage, shouting all the time, "They've all eaten macaroni – but they've forgotten me!" In vain, Catharinella tried to soothe him down, but there was nothing she could do save get away as quickly as possible with her young man. This she did, not taking a thing with her but a brush, a comb, and a mirror, to keep her hair tidy.

That night, when the ogre came home, he shouted as usual, "Catharinella, Catharinella, let your golden braids down and lift me into the house." But there was no answer. When at last he grew impatient and forced the door, the

old broom came to meet him, all tousle-haired and excited, struggling to pour out everything; but as he had said nothing else all day, he could only repeat "They've all eaten macaroni – but they've forgotten me!" The ogre grasped that something was wrong, and went around asking the other household things to tell, but all were so stuffed with food that they gave nothing away. Yet he soon got an idea of what had happened.

He tucked up his cloak, tied three knots in his long beard – so that it couldn't get in his way in running – and took up the chase. In a short time, he sighted the pair in the distance, in the magic coach. Nearer and nearer he drew, till he could reach out for Catharinella, who was just looking out of the coach window. In her panic she flung her comb at him – and in a trice it changed into iron bars, which caught the ogre's beard as he tried to get across. In the end he succeeded and almost clutched the coach; but now Catharinella flung out her brush, which instantly turned into a thorn-bush. The ogre's beard got caught again, and his cloak torn; but once more he managed to struggle through and come near the coach. Then Catharinella threw out the mirror.

It turned into a lake and drowned the ogre.

THE AUTOGRAPH

Margaret Joy

One Saturday afternoon, Mark was sitting back in an armchair feeling really upset. One leg was in a cast and it was resting on a pillow on a stool in front of him.

"I'm fed up," he said to his mother.

"Never mind," she said. "Broken legs get better, you know. Now why don't you watch football on television, while I go in the kitchen and make a cake? Shall I switch the set on for you?"

"No," frowned Mark. He was still upset. Imagine falling off his bike and breaking his leg. And it would have to happen just when his Dad and his big brother, Steve, had promised to take him to a real football game. His first real football game, in the stadium, and with Vince Oliver playing. Dad's newspaper called Vince Oliver "the fastest thing on two legs" – and the game was today, and he was going to have to miss it, because of his broken leg.

"I'm fed up," said Mark again.

"Never mind," said his Dad, "I'll bring you my program back, and I bet they'll be showing the game on TV later this evening. I'll ask Mom to let you stay up to see it."

"I'm still fed up," said Mark.

Steve came in with an ice-cream cone.

"Here you are," he said. "I've just bought it for you from Sam. He asked how you were, and I said you were fed up because you were missing the game. So he put an extra sprinkle of nuts on top and stuck an extra chocolate bar in – said it was Sam's Special and it would cheer you up."

Now Mark had to smile and began to lick the ice cream.

"We'll have to go now, son," said his Dad, coming in with his red and white scarf around his neck. "I won't forget your program."

"And I tell you what," said Steve, "I'll try to get Vince Oliver's autograph for you. His very own name, written by himself in his very own handwriting – how about that?"

Mark felt really cheerful now, and he waved goodbye to them and let his mother switch on the television for him, while he enjoyed his Sam's Special. He watched television most of that Saturday afternoon. Then his leg began to itch, and because there was a cast on it, he couldn't get at it to scratch. Then he began to get stiff from sitting in the same position in the same chair for hours on end.

"I hate this cast," he said to his mother when she came in to see how he was.

"Never mind," she said.

Everybody seems to be saying that to me today, thought Mark. But I *do* mind. I don't want a rotten old cast on my leg. I want to be at the game with Steve and Dad. I want to see Vince Oliver play.

"Will you come in the kitchen and ice the top of the cake for me, Mark?" asked his mother. "I'll let you use the icing bag to make squiggly patterns, if you like."

Mark sniffed, then cheered up and hopped into the kitchen on his good leg. He had to hold onto chairs and doorjambs to help him. Then his mother helped him up onto a high stool to do the icing.

When his Dad and Steve got home, he could see that their team had won. They both looked pleased. Dad was smiling, and Steve was chanting:

"Hooray Reds! Hooray R-e-ds!"

"Here's the program," said Dad, handing it to Mark. "We won."

"Did you see Vince Oliver?" asked Mark.

"Course," said Steve. "He got two touchdowns. Guess what, though – near the end of the game, he was tackled, and he fell against one of the goal posts. They had to help him off."

"Hey, I hope he's not badly hurt," said Mark. "So you didn't get his autograph?"

"No, sorry, I'll try next time he's playing."

But they found out later that Vince Oliver was to be out of football for some time; he had broken his arm.

Two weeks later, Mark had to go back to the hospital. The doctor wanted to see his leg and put on a new cast. He sat with his Mom in the waiting room. A nurse came in.

"Mark Foster, your turn, please."

Mark and his Mom went into a little room where another nurse cut down the side of his cast with a pair of specially strong scissors. After that, a doctor examined his leg and said it was mending beautifully. Then the nurse put fresh plaster around his leg. His Mom pushed him back to the waiting room in a wheelchair, and they sat and waited for the plaster to dry.

"Two more weeks, Mark, and you should be playing football again," smiled the nurse.

His Mom went over to her to make the next appointment for him. The man in the chair next to Mark's had his arm in plaster. He had been listening.

"Do you like football, then?" he asked.

"Oh, yes," said Mark. He told the man about how he'd been going to see his first live football game when he fell off his bike and couldn't go. "And I specially wanted to see Vince Oliver play," said Mark, "so when I had to stay at home, my brother said he'd get his autograph, but he couldn't, because Vince broke his arm."

"Yes," said the man with the arm in plaster. "Yes, I did."

"*You* did?" said Mark. He stared. "You? Are you Vince Oliver? But you're not like my pictures of you. You're not in your football things."

"No, I only wear them for training and for games," laughed Vince. "Usually I wear ordinary clothes. That's why you didn't recognize me. You're used to seeing pictures of me in red and white."

Mark was so amazed, he couldn't speak. He just stared and stared. Vince Oliver, *the* Vince Oliver, was sitting on the chair next to him. He couldn't believe it.

"Tell you what," said Vince. "I can still write with my

left hand. Would you like my autograph now – or is it too late?"

Mark could only shake his head. Vince took a pen from his pocket and bent down over Mark's leg. Mark squinted sideways to watch. Vince was writing:

"From one footballer. to another. All the best, Vince Oliver."

The plaster was taken off two weeks later. When the nurse had removed it, Mark said, "I want to keep that, please. It's my autograph from Vince."

The nurse looked very surprised, but she gave it back to him. Now it's hanging on Mark's bedroom wall for everyone to see. A little label is pinned next to it. It reads:

"The fastest thing on two legs autographed this for the slowest thing on one leg."

THE STEADFAST
TIN SOLDIER

Hans Christian Andersen

There were once twenty-five tin soldiers, all of them brothers, for they had all been made from the same tin kitchen spoon. They shouldered arms, and looked straight in front of them, very stylish in their red and blue uniforms. "Tin soldiers!" That was the very first thing that they heard in this world, when the lid of their box was taken off. A little boy had shouted this and clapped his hands; he had been given them as a birthday present, and now he set them out on the table. Each soldier was exactly like the next – except for one, which had only a single leg; he was the last to be molded, and there was not quite enough tin left. Yet he stood just as well on his one leg as the others did on their two, and he is this story's hero.

On the table where they were placed, there were many other toys, but the one that everyone noticed first was a paper castle. Through its little windows, you could see right into the rooms. In front of it, tiny trees were arranged around a piece of mirror, which was meant to look like a lake. Swans made of wax seemed to float on its surface, and gaze at their white reflections. The whole scene was enchanting – and the prettiest thing of all was a girl who stood in the open doorway; she too was cut out of paper, but her gauzy skirt was of finest tulle; a narrow blue ribbon crossed her shoulder like a scarf and was held by a shining sequin almost the size of her face. This charming little creature held both of her arms stretched out, for she was a dancer; indeed, one of her legs was raised so high in the air that the tin soldier could not see it at all; he thought that she had only one leg like himself.

"Now, she would be just the right wife for me," he thought. "But she is so grand; she lives in a castle, and I have only a box – and there are five-and-twenty of us in that! There certainly isn't room for her. Still, I can try to make her acquaintance." So he lay down full-length behind a snuffbox which was on the table; from there, he could easily watch the little paper dancer, who continued to stand on one leg without losing her balance.

When evening came, all the other tin soldiers were put in their box, and the children went to bed. Now the toys began to have games of their own; they played visiting, and school, and battles, and going to parties. The tin soldiers rattled in their box, for they wanted to join in, but they couldn't get the lid off. The nutcrackers turned somersaults, and the slate pencil squeaked on the slate; there was such a din that the canary woke up and took part in the talk – what's more, he did it in verse. The only two who didn't move were the tin soldier and the little dancer; she continued to stand on the point of her toe, with her arms held out; he stood just as steadily on his single leg – and never once did he take his eyes from her.

Now the clock struck twelve. Crack! – the lid flew off the snuffbox and up popped a little black goblin. There was no

snuff inside the box – it was a kind of trick, a jack-in-the-box.

"Tin soldier!" screeched the goblin. "Keep your eyes to yourself!"

But the tin soldier pretended not to hear.

"All right, just you wait till tomorrow!" said the goblin.

When morning came and the children were up again, the tin soldier was placed on the window ledge. The goblin may have been responsible, or perhaps a draft blowing through – anyhow, the window suddenly swung open, and out fell the tin soldier, all the three stories to the ground. It was a dreadful fall! His leg pointed up, his head was down, and he came to a halt with his bayonet stuck between the paving stones.

The servant-girl and the little boy went to search in the street, but although they were almost treading on the soldier, they somehow failed to see him. If he had called out, "Here I am!" they would have found him easily, but he didn't think it proper behavior to cry out when he was in uniform.

Now it began to rain; the drops fell fast – it was a drenching shower. When it was over, a pair of urchins passed. "Look!" said one of them. "There's a tin soldier. Let's put him out to sea."

So they made a boat out of newspaper and put the tin soldier in the middle, and set it in the fast-flowing gutter at the edge of the street. Away he sped, and the two boys ran beside him clapping their hands. Goodness, what waves there were in that gutter-stream, what rolling tides! It had been a real downpour. The paper boat tossed up and down, sometimes whirling round and round, until the soldier felt quite giddy. But he remained as steadfast as ever, not moving a muscle, still looking straight in front of him, still shouldering arms.

All at once, the boat entered a tunnel under the sidewalk. Oh, it was dark, quite as dark as it was in the box at home. "Wherever am I going now?" the tin soldier wondered. "Yes, it must be the goblin's doing. Ah! If only that young lady were here with me in the boat, I wouldn't care if it were twice as dark."

Suddenly, from its home in the tunnel, out rushed a large water rat. "Have you a passport?" it demanded. "No entry without a passport!"

But the tin soldier said never a word; he only gripped his musket more tightly than ever. The boat rushed onward, and behind it rushed the rat in fast pursuit. Ugh! How it ground its teeth and yelled to the sticks and straws, "Stop him! Stop him! He hasn't paid his toll! He hasn't shown his passport!"

There was no stopping the boat, though, for the stream ran stronger and stronger. The tin soldier could just see a bright glimpse of daylight far ahead where the end of the tunnel must be, but at the same time, he heard a roaring noise which well might have frightened a bolder man. Just imagine! At the end of the tunnel, the stream thundered down into a great canal. It was as dreadful for him as a plunge down a giant waterfall would be for us.

But how could he stop? Already he was close to the terrible edge. The boat raced on, and the poor tin soldier held himself as stiffly as he could – no one could say of him that he even blinked an eye.

Suddenly the little vessel whirled around three or four times, and filled with water right to the brim; what could it do but sink! The tin soldier stood in water up to his neck; deeper and deeper sank the boat, softer and softer grew the paper, until at last the water closed over the soldier's head. He thought of the lovely little dancer whom he would never see again, and in his ears rang the words of a song:

> "Onward, onward, warrior brave!
> Fear not danger, nor the grave."

Then the paper boat collapsed entirely. Out fell the tin soldier – and he was promptly swallowed up by a fish.

Oh, how dark it was in the fish's stomach! It was even worse than the tunnel and very much more cramped. But the tin soldier's courage remained unchanged; there he lay, as steadfast as ever, his musket still at his shoulder. The fish swam wildly about, twisted and turned, and then became

quite still. Something flashed through like a streak of lightning – then all around was cheerful daylight, and a voice cried out, "The tin soldier!"

The fish had been caught, taken to market, sold, and carried into the kitchen, where the cook had cut it open with a large knife. Now she picked up the soldier, holding him around his waist between her finger and thumb, and took him into the living room, so that all the family could see the remarkable character who had traveled around inside a fish. But the tin soldier was not at all proud. They stood him up on the table, and there – well, the world is full of wonders! – he saw that he was in the very same room where his adventures had started; there were the very same children; there were the very same toys; there was the fine paper castle with the graceful little dancer at the door. She was still poised on one leg, with the other raised high in the air. Ah, she was steadfast too. The tin soldier was deeply

moved; he would have liked to weep tin tears, only that would not have been soldierly behavior. He looked at her, and she looked at him, but not a word passed between them.

And then a strange thing happened. One of the small boys picked up the tin soldier and threw him into the stove. He had no reason for doing this; it must have been the snuffbox goblin's fault.

The tin soldier stood framed in a blaze of light. The heat was intense, but whether this came from the fire or his burning love, he could not tell. His bright colors were now gone – but whether they had been washed away by his journey, or through his sorrow, none could say. He looked at the pretty little dancer, and she looked at him; he felt that he was melting away, but he still stood steadfast, shouldering arms. Suddenly the door flew open; a gust of air caught the little paper girl, and she flew like a sylph right into the stove, straight to the waiting tin soldier; there she flashed into flame and vanished.

The soldier presently melted down to a lump of tin, and the next day, when the maid raked out the ashes she found him – in the shape of a little tin heart. And the dancer? All that they found was her sequin, and that was as black as soot.

JACK AND THE BEANSTALK

Joseph Jacobs

There was once upon a time a poor widow who had an only son named Jack, and a cow named Milky-white. And all they had to live on was the milk the cow gave every morning, which they carried to the market and sold. But one morning Milky-white gave no milk, and they didn't know what to do.

"What shall we do, what shall we do?" said the widow, wringing her hands.

"Cheer up, mother, I'll go and get work somewhere," said Jack.

"We've tried that before, and nobody would take you," said his mother. "We must sell Milky-white and with the money start a shop, or something."

"All right, mother," says Jack; "it's market day today, and I'll soon sell Milky-white, and then we'll see what we can do."

So he took the cow's halter in his hand, and off he

started. He hadn't gone far when he met a funny-looking old man, who said to him: "Good morning, Jack."

"Good morning to you," said Jack, and wondered how he knew his name.

"Well, Jack, and where are you off to?" said the man.

"I'm going to market to sell our cow here."

"You look the proper sort of chap to sell cows," said the man; "and do you know how many beans make five?"

"Two in each hand and one in your mouth," says Jack, as sharp as a needle.

"Right you are," says the man, "and here they are, the very beans themselves," he went on, pulling out of his pocket a number of strange-looking beans. "As you are so sharp," says he, "I don't mind doing a swap with you – your cow for these beans."

"Go along," says Jack.

"Ah! you don't know what these beans are," said the man. "If you plant them overnight, by morning they grow right up to the sky."

"Really?" said Jack. "You don't say so."

"Yes, that is so, and if it doesn't turn out to be true, you can have your cow back."

"Right," says Jack and hands him Milky-white's halter and pockets the beans.

Back goes Jack home, and as he hadn't gone very far, it wasn't dusk by the time he got to his door.

"Back already, Jack?" said his mother. "I see you haven't got Milky-white, so you've sold her. How much did you get for her?"

"You'll never guess, mother," says Jack.

"No, you don't say. Good boy! Five, ten, fifteen, no, it can't be twenty."

"I told you you couldn't guess. What do you say to these beans; they're magical, plant them overnight and –"

"What!" says Jack's mother, "have you been such a fool, such a dolt, such an idiot, as to give away my Milky-white, the best milker in the parish, and prime beef to boot, for a set of paltry beans? Take that! Take that! Take that! And as for your precious beans, here they go out of the window. And now off with you to bed. Not a sup shall you drink, and not a bit shall you swallow this very night."

So Jack went upstairs to his little room in the attic, and sad and sorry he was, to be sure, as much for his mother's sake, as for the loss of his supper.

At last, he dropped off to sleep.

When he woke up, the room looked so funny. The sun

was shining into part of it, and yet all the rest was quite dark and shady. So Jack jumped up and dressed himself and went to the window. And what do you think he saw? Why, the beans his mother had thrown out of the window into the garden had sprung up into a big beanstalk that went up and up and up till it reached the sky. So the man spoke truth after all.

The beanstalk grew up quite close past Jack's window, so all he had to do was to open it and jump onto the beanstalk, which ran up just like a big ladder. So Jack climbed, and he climbed and he climbed and he climbed and he climbed and he climbed and he climbed till at last he reached the sky. And when he got there, he found a long broad road going as straight as a dart. So he walked along and he walked along and he walked along, till he came to a great big tall house, and on the doorstep there was a great big tall woman.

"Good morning, m'am," says Jack, quite polite-like. "Could you be so kind as to give me some breakfast?" For he hadn't had anything to eat, you know, the night before and was as hungry as a hunter.

"It's breakfast you want, is it?" says the great big tall woman. "It's breakfast you'll be if you don't move off from here. My man is an ogre, and there's nothing he likes better than boys broiled on toast. You'd better be moving on, or he'll soon be coming."

"Oh! please, m'am, do give me something to eat, m'am. I've had nothing to eat since yesterday morning, really and truly, m'am," says Jack. "I may as well be broiled as die of hunger."

Well, the ogre's wife was not half so bad after all. So she

took Jack into the kitchen, and gave him a hunk of bread and cheese and a pitcher of milk. But Jack hadn't half finished these when thump! thump! thump! the whole house began to tremble with the noise of someone coming.

"Goodness gracious me! It's my old man," said the ogre's wife, "what on earth shall I do? Come along quick and jump in here." And she bundled Jack into the oven just as the ogre came in.

He was a big one, to be sure. At his belt, he had three calves strung up by the heels, and he unhooked them and threw them down on the table and said: "Here, wife, broil me a couple of these for breakfast. Ah! what's this I smell?

"Fee-fi-fo-fum,
I smell the blood of an Englishman,
Be he alive, or be he dead
I'll have his bones to grind my bread."

"Nonsense, dear," said his wife, "you're dreaming. Or perhaps you smell the scraps of that little boy you liked so much for yesterday's dinner. Here, you go and have a wash and clean up, and by the time you come back, your breakfast'll be ready for you."

So off the ogre went, and Jack was just going to jump out of the oven and run away when the woman told him not. "Wait till he's asleep," says she; "he always has a doze after breakfast."

Well, the ogre had his breakfast, and after that he goes to a big chest and takes out of it a couple of bags of gold, and down he sits and counts till at last his head began to nod and he began to snore till the whole house shook again.

Then Jack crept out on tiptoe from his oven; and as he was passing the ogre, he took one of the bags of gold under

his arm, and off he pelters till he came to the beanstalk, and then he threw down the bag of gold, which, of course, fell into his mother's garden, and then he climbed down till at last he got home and told his mother and showed her the gold and said: "Well, mother, wasn't I right about the beans? They are really magical, you see."

So they lived on the bag of gold for some time, but at last they came to the end of it, and Jack made up his mind to try his luck once more at the top of the beanstalk. So one fine morning, he rose up early, and got on to the beanstalk, and he climbed and he climbed and he climbed and he climbed and he climbed and he climbed till at last he came out onto the road again and up to the great big tall house he had been to before. There, sure enough, was the great big tall woman a-standing on the doorstep.

"Good morning, m'am," says Jack, as bold as brass, "could you be so good as to give me something to eat?"

"Go away, my boy," said the big tall woman, "or else my man will eat you up for breakfast. But aren't you the youngster who came here once before? Do you know, that very day, my man missed one of his bags of gold."

"That's strange, m'am," said Jack, "I dare say I could tell you something about that, but I'm so hungry I can't speak till I've had something to eat."

Well, the big tall woman was so curious that she took him in and gave him something to eat. But he had scarcely begun munching it as slowly as he could when thump! thump! they heard the giant's footstep, and his wife hid Jack away in the oven.

All happened as it did before. In came the ogre as he did before, said: "Fe-fi-fo-fum," and had his breakfast of three broiled oxen. Then he said: "Wife, bring me the hen that lays the golden eggs." So she brought it, and the ogre said: "Lay," and it laid an egg all of gold. And then the ogre began to nod his head and to snore till the house shook.

Then Jack crept out of the oven on tiptoe and caught hold of the golden hen, and was off before you could say "Jack Robinson." But this time the hen gave a cackle which woke the ogre, and just as Jack got out of the house, he

heard him calling: "Wife, wife, what have you done with my golden hen?"

And the wife said: "Why, my dear?"

But that was all Jack heard, for he rushed off to the beanstalk and climbed down like a house on fire. And when he got home he showed his mother the hen and said "Lay" to it; and it laid a golden egg every time he said "Lay."

Well, Jack was not content, and it wasn't very long before he determined to have another try at his luck up there at the top of the beanstalk. So one fine morning, he rose up early, and got onto the beanstalk, and he climbed and he climbed and he climbed and he climbed till he got to the top. But this time he knew better than to go straight to the ogre's house. And when he got near it, he waited behind a bush till he saw the ogre's wife come out with a pail to get some water, and then he crept into the house and got into the cooking pot. He hadn't been there long when he heard thump! thump! thump! as before, and in came the ogre and his wife.

"Fee-fi-fo-fum, I smell the blood of an Englishman," cried out the ogre. "I smell him, wife, I smell him."

"Do you, my dearie?" says the ogre's wife. "Then, if it's that little rogue that stole your gold and the hen that laid the golden eggs he's sure to have got into the oven." And they both rushed to the oven. But Jack wasn't there, luckily, and the ogre's wife said: "There you are again with your fee-fi-fo-fum. Why, of course, it's the boy you caught last night that I've just broiled for your breakfast. How forgetful I am, and how careless you are not to know the difference between live and dead after all these years."

So the ogre sat down to the breakfast and ate it, but

every now and then, he would mutter: "Well, I could have sworn –" and he'd get up and search the pantry and the cupboards and everything, only, luckily, he didn't think of the cooking pot.

After breakfast was over, the ogre called out: "Wife, wife, bring me my golden harp." So she brought it and put it on the table before him. Then he said: "Sing!" and the golden harp sang most beautifully. And it went on singing, till the ogre fell asleep and began to snore like thunder.

Then Jack lifted up the pot lid very quietly and got down like a mouse and crept on hands and knees till he came to the table, when up he crawled, caught hold of the golden harp and dashed with it toward the door. But the harp called out quite loud: "Master! Master!," and the ogre woke up just in time to see Jack running off with his harp.

Jack ran as fast as he could, and the ogre came rushing after and would soon have caught him, only Jack had a start and dodged him a bit and knew where he was going. When he got to the beanstalk, the ogre was no more than twenty yards away when, suddenly, he saw Jack disappear, and when he came to the end of the road, he saw Jack underneath climbing down for dear life. Well, the ogre didn't like trusting himself to such a ladder, and he stood and waited, so Jack got another start. But just then the harp cried out: "Master! Master!," and the ogre swung himself down onto the beanstalk, which shook with his weight. Down climbs Jack, and after him climbed the ogre. By this time, Jack had climbed down and climbed down and climbed down till he was very nearly home. So he called out: "Mother! Mother! bring me an ax, bring me an ax." And his mother came rushing out with the ax in her hand, but when she came to the beanstalk, she stood stock still with fright, for there she saw the ogre with his legs just through the clouds.

But Jack jumped down and got hold of the ax and gave a chop at the beanstalk which cut it half in two. The ogre felt the beanstalk shake and quiver, so he stopped to see what was the matter. Then Jack gave another chop with the ax, and the beanstalk was cut in two and began to topple over. The ogre fell down and broke his crown, and the beanstalk came toppling after.

Then Jack showed his mother his golden harp, and what with showing that and selling the golden eggs, Jack and his mother became very rich, and he married a great princess, and they lived happy ever after.

PUSS IN BOOTS

Charles Perrault

Many, many years ago, there lived a miller who had a mill, a donkey, a cat, and three sons. So when he died, it was very simple to divide up his belongings. The mill went to the eldest son, the donkey went to the second son, and to the youngest son went the cat.

As you might imagine, the youngest son was not happy about this. He grumbled about it to himself. "What am I going to do?" he wondered. "I've nothing but a cat for my fortune. It's all very well for my brothers. With the mill and the donkey, they'll earn their living well enough. But what about me?"

Now, the cat overheard what his master was saying, and to the young man's astonishment, he spoke. "Don't worry, master," he said. "You won't starve. I have a plan."

"You have a plan?" cried the young man. "But what can you do?"

"Never mind about that, master," said the cat. "All I shall need is a sack . . . and a pair of boots. Ask no more questions. Do as I ask, and you'll find you're not half as badly off as you thought."

The youngest son remembered that the cat had always been extraordinarily clever; that is, when it came to catching rats or mice. He'd seen the cat lying in the flourbin, pretending to be dead . . . until a rat came unwisely to nibble at the flour. It was impossible to imagine a cat more clever at that sort of trick. If he took the cat's advice, it could hardly make things worse. So he did what the cat asked; and the cat pulled the boots on, slung the sack over his shoulder, and set off along the road.

He made for a field, went into the brambles at the edge of it, and picked some thistles. The boots protected his feet from the sharp thorns. He put the thistles in the sack and laid the sack down near the entrance to a rabbit burrow. The mouth of the sack was wide open. Then the cat stretched out on the ground as if he were dead.

In a moment or so, out of the burrow came a young rabbit. He caught sight of the thistles in the sack, and jumped in. In a flash, the cat came to life; he pulled the cord at the mouth of the sack, and the rabbit was caught. Then off went the cat to the town, which was the biggest town in the country; and the biggest building in the town was the palace, where the king lived.

The sentry at the palace gate looked at the cat suspiciously. "Halt!" he cried. "What do you want, cat?"

The cat said, "You see this sack over my shoulder? In it there's a present for the king – a plump young rabbit."

"Oh," said the sentry. "Is there? Well, the king isn't in the habit of being visited by cats, even if they're bringing him presents."

"By ordinary cats, I guess not," said the cat. "But what about cats wearing fine boots, like these of mine?"

The sentry, who was not very bright, became confused. "Fine boots?" he said. "What's that got to do with it? Oh, well. All right, then. In you go. But I really don't know if it's the right thing to do . . ."

And while the sentry stood there, looking uneasy and biting his lip, the cat slipped past him and soon was standing before the king. The cat bowed low and laid the sack at the king's feet. "Your Majesty," he said, "this sack contains a very fine plump young rabbit. It is for you."

"Ah, yes," said the king, who wasn't particularly bright either. "Oh. We thank you for it, cat."

"Oh, don't thank me, Your Majesty," said the cat. "The gift is from my master, the Marquis of Carabas."

The king was more confused than the sentry had been. "Oh," he said. "The Marquis of Carabas, eh? Well, my young – er – friend, give your master the Marquis of Carabas our thanks and tell him that his present gives us the greatest pleasure."

So off went the cat, back to his master. But he told the young man nothing of what had happened.

The next day, off he went again. This time, he lay down in a cornfield as if he were dead, leaving the sack full of thistles on the ground and with its mouth wide open. In no time, two partridges had flown down straight into the sack. The cat came to life, pulled the strings in the mouth of the sack, and trapped the birds inside. And off he went again to the palace. Once more, he was halted by the sentry.

"Halt!" cried the sentry. "What's your . . .? Oh, it's you, is it, Master Cat?"

"It is, indeed," said the cat. "Today, I have two plump partridges for the king."

"Two partridges!" cried the sentry. "What's that got to do with – Oh, very well, in you go. Though if it's the right thing to do, I . . ."

But the cat didn't wait to hear what the sentry had to say – which was just as well, because the sentry, now very confused, went on saying it for half an hour or more. Into the palace the cat went, and stood again before the king. He bowed low and laid the sack at the king's feet.

"Your Majesty," he said, "this sack contains two fine plump partridges – for you!"

"And from your master again?" asked the king. "The Marquis of – er –"

"Of Carabas, Your Majesty," said the cat.

"Ah, yes, yes, yes," said the king, who'd never heard of such a Marquis, but didn't like to say so. "Yes, a most excellent nobleman. Hmm – where do the partridges come from, Master Cat?"

"From my master's own hunting grounds, Your Majesty," said the cat. "His *vast* hunting grounds."

"Oh, quite," said the king. "Well, thank the Marquis for us, Master Cat. And for yourself, take these few pieces of gold."

"Your Majesty is too kind," said the cat.

"Not at all. Delighted," said the king. "Most generous of your master. Excellent nobleman. Marquis of –"

"Carabas, Your Majesty," said the cat.

"Marquis of Carabas, yes," said the king. "Yes, yes . . ."

But the cat didn't wait to hear the rest of what the king said – which was just as well, for the king went on muttering the name of the Marquis of Carabas, and saying he was an excellent nobleman, and wondering who on earth he was, for half an hour or more. But the cat bowed and left the room.

Back home, he again told his young master nothing of what had happened; but the few pieces of gold were enough to buy good meals for both of them.

And so it went on. Day after day, for two or three months, the cat took gifts to the king; and every time, he told the king that they had come from his master's hunting grounds. And every time the king said how grateful he was to this . . . Marquis of Carabas he had never met.

But one day, the sentry told the cat that if he came with a gift for the king the following day, he would come in vain. "You see, Master Cat," said the sentry, who was now on very good terms with the cat, though he was still puzzled by the whole thing, "you see, tomorrow the king is going out for a long drive with his daughter. The loveliest princess in the world, Master Cat."

"Really?" said the cat, pricking up his ears. "Oh, *really!* Of course, their route – the way they're going on their drive – that's a secret, naturally?"

"Oh, no, it's no secret," said the sentry. "They're going all the way along the river bank. You're looking very thoughtful, Master Cat."

"Oh," said the cat. "I was only thinking that . . . I must remember not to call at the palace tomorrow. Thank you, sentry. Good day."

And he hurried home, purring to himself with delight and glee. He *had* been thinking – but it *wasn't* about not calling at the palace next day. As soon as he got home, he cried, "Master! Master! If you follow my advice now, your fortune is made! All you have to do is to come with me tomorrow and swim in the river. I'll do the rest."

You might have expected the miller's son to say he'd do nothing of the sort! Swim in the river in order to come into a fortune! The cat must be mad! But by now, the young man knew that, whatever was going on, he was master of perhaps the cleverest cat in the world. Well, what other cat had ever come home with gold to buy food with? So the miller's son said, "All right. I don't know what you're up to. But I'll do what you say."

"Good," said the cat. "There is one other small thing,

master. If anyone should address you by some strange name – the Marquis of Something–or–other, perhaps – don't look surprised. Whatever you do, *don't* look surprised! And *don't* say it isn't you!"

The miller's son laughed, a little uneasily. "Very well," he said. "But I hope these tricks of yours won't lead us into any trouble."

So, next day, the young man went with the cat down to the river. He undressed and plunged into the water to swim. The cat went at once to a large stone on the river bank and hid something underneath it. At that moment came the sound of carriage wheels and horses' hooves, and the sound of horns. The king was coming, with the princess beside him in his golden carriage. The cat dashed onto the road and began shouting at the top of his voice, "Help! Help! My master is drowning! The Marquis of Carabas is drowning!"

The king looked out of the carriage and recognized the cat. At once, he ordered the carriage to stop, and his guards to run to the river and save the Marquis. The guards leaped from their horses, rushed down to the water, and pulled the cat's bewildered young master out of the water. Meanwhile the cat approached the carriage and, bowing deeply, said, "Oh, Your Majesty! Not only was my master drowning, but while he was in the water thieves came and made off with his clothes. Oh, what an unlucky day!"

"This is dreadful!" cried the king. "Quite dreadful! The Marquis must not go without clothes! Guard! Go at once to the palace, and bring the finest suit from our wardrobe for My Lord the Marquis of Carabas! On the double!"

The truth is, of course, that the shabby clothes belonging

to the cat's master had not been stolen. They were what the cat had hidden under that large stone.

The guard was soon back with a fine suit of clothes; and when the miller's son was dressed in them, he looked very handsome, and every inch a nobleman. The cat introduced him to the king. "Your Majesty – my master, the Marquis of Carabas!"

"My Lord Marquis," cried the king, "we are delighted to meet you at last. This is our daughter, the princess. And now, My Lord Marquis, it would give us the greatest pleasure if you would join us in the carriage and accompany us on our drive."

And with a blowing of horns and snorting of horses, and a fine sound of horses' hooves, off they went.

"But where, My Lord Marquis," said the king, "is that excellent servant of yours, the cat?"

"I – I think I see him, Your Majesty," said the miller's son. "He's hurrying ahead of us there in the distance." The young man, of course, had no idea what the cat was up to. So he said, "He has my orders, Your Majesty, and is busy carrying them out."

"Ah, yes, indeed," said the king, and the carriage sped on. The miller's son shyly looked at the princess and thought she was beautiful, and the princess shyly looked at the miller's son and thought he was handsome.

Meanwhile, the cat was hurrying along the road well in front of the royal carriage. He came to a meadow that was being mowed and hurried over to speak to the mowers.

"Good morning, my dear good mowers," he cried.

"Mornin', Master Cat," said the mowers.

"I have a message for you," said the cat. "The king is coming this way, and he's bound to ask you whose meadow you are mowing."

"Ah," said the mowers.

"You must reply," said the cat, "that the meadow belongs to My Lord the Marquis of Carabas. Can you remember that?"

"But – Master Cat . . . !" cried the mowers.

"I'm afraid," said the cat, "that if you don't do this it will be necessary to have you all chopped up into mincemeat."

"Into what?" cried the mowers.

"Oh! Mincemeat! Mincemeat! Mincemeat!" cried the cat, impatiently. "Surely you know what mincemeat is!"

"Ah, mincemeat," said the mowers. "Well, in that case,

Master Cat, we will certainly do as you say. Marquis of –"

"Carabas," said the cat.

"Ah, yes, Carabas," said the mowers. "Otherwise . . ."

"Mincemeat," said the cat.

"Ah yes," said the mowers. "We will do what you ask, Master Cat."

The cat hurried off, and the mowers went on with their work, trembling at the thought of what the cat had threatened. Soon they heard the sound of the royal carriage; and, as the cat had foreseen, it drew up beside the meadow. "This is a huge meadow you are mowing, my men," called the king. "To whom does this huge meadow belong?"

"Ah, Your Majesty, this huge meadow, Your Majesty, ah, yes, Your Majesty," cried the mowers, feeling very anxious. "It belongs, Your Majesty, to the Marquis of – er – Carabas."

"The Marquis of Carabas!" cried the king, turning to the miller's son. "So it is your land, My Lord?"

"Ah, yes, indeed," said the cat's master. He was becoming very confused, but he remembered what the cat had told him. He must say yes to everything. "Of course. I believe it is my land."

"Hmm," said the king. "Very fine land! Well, well . . . drive on . . ."

Meanwhile, the cat had come to a cornfield that was being harvested. He bustled up to the harvesters.

"Good morning, my dear good harvesters," he cried.

"Mornin', Master Cat," said the harvesters.

"I bring you a message," said the cat. "The king is coming this way in his carriage. He is certain to ask whose cornfield this is that you are harvesting. I want you to reply that the cornfield belongs to My Lord the Marquis of Carabas. You understand?"

"But – Master Cat – !" cried the harvesters.

"Now, should you fail to do this," said the cat, briskly, "I should be forced, of course, to have you all chopped up into mincemeat."

"Into mincemeat, Master Cat?"

"That's what I said. Mincemeat!"

"Oh," said the harvesters, who hated the idea of being chopped up into mincemeat. "Oh, we'll tell the king, never you fear, Master Cat."

So the cat hurried off, and the harvesters went on with their work. A few moments later, the royal carriage arrived, with a great sound of wheels and hooves and horns.

"Good morning, harvesters," called the king. "To whom does this splendid large field belong?"

"Ah, it belongs," said the harvesters, "er – to My Lord the Marquis of – Car – er – ab – er – as, Your Majesty. The Marquis of Carabas."

And as before, the king was astonished and delighted, and again he congratulated the miller's son on having such splendid fields. And so it went on. The cat always hurried ahead, and to all those he met he said the same thing: in cornfield and meadow, in pasture and by mill-stream, everywhere the cat gave his orders: and everywhere the king was told that this field or stream or mill belonged to the Marquis of Carabas.

And now the cat, hurrying ahead, had reached the foot of a high hill, on the top of which stood a large and splendid castle. There was an old woman coming down the hill, and the cat called to her. "Old woman, good day to you," he cried. "Tell me, who lives in the castle up there?"

"My master lives there," said the old woman. "Tell me, how far have you come, Master Cat?"

"I have come many miles along the river bank," said the cat. "Through many cornfields and meadows and pastures and by many mills."

"Well, everything you have seen on that journey," said the old woman, "belongs to my master. Of all the ogres in the world –"

"He's an ogre then, old woman?"

"Oh, he is indeed, a very wicked ogre. But as I was saying, of all the ogres in the world, he is the richest. And he's the cleverest, too. He has the power of turning himself into any animal he has a mind to. Oh, he is clever – and terrible. Terrible, Master Cat!" And she cackled, as if it pleased her to think how terrible her master was.

"Well, thank you, old woman," said the cat thoughtfully: and he made his way up the hill to the great door of the castle. And there he tugged at the bell.

A servant opened the door, wearing a fine uniform. "What do you want, Master Cat?" he asked.

"I have come a long way to see your master and pay my respects to him," said the cat. "I would consider it the *greatest* honor to have a word or two with an ogre so *famous* and so *clever*. If you would repeat those words exactly to your master –"

A moment later, the cat was shown into the great room where the ogre was sitting. "You wish," said the ogre, who was obviously pleased to have been told that the cat thought him famous and clever, "to have the honor of speaking to me, they tell me."

"Indeed, Master, that is an honor in itself," the cat replied. "But there is a greater honor that, alas, I can hardly hope for."

"And what is that?" asked the ogre.

"I have heard," said the cat, "that you have a remarkable power of changing yourself into all sorts of animals."

"That is so," said the ogre.

"Forgive me," said the cat, "but I can hardly believe it."

"I will prove it to you with the greatest of pleasure," said the delighted ogre. "Watch! I'll turn myself into –"

"May I suggest –" said the cat hastily.

"A lion!" said the ogre.

"A lion!" cried the cat. "Oh, my goodness! Oh, yes, I

see! So you are! I mean, so you have! I mean," said the cat, backing into the corner of the room, "I see you have turned yourself into a lion! Oh, dear!"

"And back again to myself," said the ogre, to the cat's relief. "That gave you quite a fright, eh?"

"Ha, ha!" said the cat, pretending to be amazed. "Yes, quite a fright! An astonishing trick! But I've heard that you can also turn yourself into a very small animal, like a rat . . . or a mouse . . . Now, that I do find hard to believe! You are such a fine large ogre – I can't quite see how you could become anything so very small as a mouse."

"Why, that's easy! It's amazingly easy!" cried the ogre. "Just you watch!" And at once, the immense ogre became a tiny mouse, scampering across the floor of the room. In a flash, the cat was on him. Never in all his years at the mill had he sprung faster than he now sprang across the great

floor of the ogre's room. One flash, one gulp, and the mouse had gone.

And at that very moment came a sound from the roadway outside the castle: wheels, hooves, horns. The royal carriage had arrived. It drew to a halt outside the door of the castle. Then came the sound of the bell. At once, the cat flashed along the great corridors, drew the bolt of the huge door, and swung it open. Out he ran and bowed low to the king.

"Welcome, Your Majesty," he cried, "to the castle."

"Why," cried the king, turning to the miller's son. "This is your cat, your servant, My Lord Marquis."

If the miller's son had not been wearing a fine feathered hat from the king's wardrobe, his hair would have stood on end. He didn't know *what* was going on! But he managed to say, "Ah, yes, it is, Your Majesty. Indeed, that is my servant, the cat."

"Who else should it be," said the cat, who looked as pleased as if he'd just swallowed a mouse (which, of course, he had), "since this is the castle of My Lord the Marquis of Carabas."

"What, My Lord!" cried the king. "This great castle is yours, too? Let us go inside at once!"

And in they went, up great stone steps to a fine hall. There, a magnificent feast was waiting for them. Actually, it had been prepared by the ogre for some of his friends who were to visit him that day: but as they approached the castle, they'd seen the King's carriage standing in front and had not dared to come in.

The cat bowed low and said, "Your Majesty, you see now why I ran ahead of your carriage. It was so that I might

reach the castle first and have this feast prepared for you
and the princess and my master."

And so the feasting began. The king sat at the head of
the table, and the cat gave orders to the ogre's servants,
who brought in the food and the wine. The servants said
nothing, then or ever after, about the ogre, for the cat had
commanded them to be silent. What threat he used, I can't
say for certain, though I believe the word mincemeat came
into it. And that is almost all of this story, except that the
king made a speech.

"Hem – er – my friends," he began. "I have been – er –
quite astonished today by what I have seen of the – er – vast
lands and possessions of the Marquis of Carabas. Now, I
think it would be safe, My Lord Marquis, to say (for I've
been watching you both in the carriage) that you admire

my daughter: and just as safe, I'm sure, to say that – er – she greatly admires you. In short, you have but to say the word, and – er – the hand of the princess in marriage is yours."

And so it was. On that very same day, the miller's son who had become the Marquis of Carabas was married to the king's daughter, and so became a prince.

And that, I think, is the whole story. Oh, yes, the cat. He was made, by his grateful master, a lord himself – not quite a marquis, but very nearly. From then on, he hunted mice only now and then, for fun. And, as befitted a great lord, he wore boots for the rest of his life.

THE OLD WOMAN WHO LIVED IN A VINEGAR BOTTLE

Elizabeth Clark

Once upon a time, there was an Old Woman who lived in a Vinegar bottle; (she had a little ladder to go in and out by). She lived there for a great many years, but after a time she grew discontented (and wouldn't you – if you lived in a Vinegar bottle?). And one day, she began to grumble, and she grumbled so loud that a Fairy, who was passing by, heard her.

"Oh, dear! Oh, dear! Oh, dear!" she said. "I oughtn't to live in a Vinegar bottle. 'Tis a shame, so it is, 'tis a shame. I ought to live in a nice little white house, with pink curtains at the windows and roses and honeysuckle growing over it, and there ought to be flowers, and vegetables in the garden, and a pig in a sty. So there ought. 'Tis a shame, so it is, 'tis a shame."

Well, the Fairy was sorry for her (and wouldn't you be sorry for a person who lived in a Vinegar bottle?). And she said, "Well, never you mind. But when you go to bed tonight, just you turn around three times, and when you wake up in the morning, you'll see what you'll see!"

So the Old Woman went to bed in the Vinegar bottle, and she turned around three times. (I don't know how there was room to do it.) And when she woke up in the morning, she was in a little white bed in a room with pink curtains. And she jumped out of bed and ran across the room and pulled aside the pink curtains and looked out of the window. And it was a little white house, with roses and honeysuckle, and there was a garden with flowers and vegetables, and she could hear a pig – grunting in the sty!

Well, the Old Woman was pleased. But she never thought to say "Thank you" to the Fairy.

Well, the Fairy, she went East and she went West, and she went North and she went South; and one day, she came back to where the Old Woman was living in the little white house with pink curtains at the windows, and roses and honeysuckle and flowers – and vegetables in the garden – and the pig in the sty. And the Fairy said to herself, "I'll just go and take a look at her. She will be pleased."

But do you know, as the Fairy passed by the Old Woman's window, she could hear the Old Woman talking to herself, and what do you think she was saying? "Oh! 'tis a shame," said the Old Woman, "'tis a shame. So it is, 'tis a shame. Why should I live in a poky little cottage? Other folks live in little red brick houses on the edge of the town where they can watch who goes by to market. Why shouldn't I live in a little red brick house on the edge of the town and see the folks going by to market? And I'm getting too old to do my own work. I ought to have a little maid to wait on me. So I did. Oh! 'tis a shame, 'tis a shame."

Well, the Fairy was disappointed because she did hope she would have been pleased. But she said, "Well, never you mind. When you go to bed tonight, just you turn around three times; and when you wake up in the morning, you'll see what you'll see!"

So the Old Woman went to bed in the little white house with the pink curtains at the windows and the roses and honeysuckle and flowers – and the vegetables in the garden – and the pig in the sty. And she turned around three times. And when she woke up in the morning – someone was standing by the bed, saying, "Please, m'am, I've brought you a cup o' tea." And when she opened her eyes and looked, there was a little maid to help her do her work; and she'd brought the Old Woman a cup of tea to drink before she got out of bed. And when the Old Woman had drunk her tea, she got up and looked out of the window. And it was a little red brick house, and it was on the edge of the town, and she could see the folk going by to market!

Well, the Old Woman was pleased. But she never thought to say "Thank you" to the Fairy.

Well, the Fairy, she went East and she went West, and she went North and she went South; and one day, she came back to where the Old Woman was living in the little red brick house, on the edge of the town, and where she could see the folks going by to market. And the Fairy said to herself, "I'll just go and take a look at her. She will be so pleased!"

But do you know, when the Fairy stood on the Old Woman's doorstep, she could hear (through the keyhole) the Old Woman talking to herself. (The Fairy wasn't listening at the keyhole. It was just as high as her ear, and she couldn't help hearing.) And what do you think she was saying? "Oh! 'tis a shame," said the Old Woman, "'tis a shame, so it is, 'tis a shame. Why should I live in a little house, when other folks live in a big house in the middle of town, with white steps up to the door, and men and maids to wait on them, and a carriage and pair to go driving in? Why shouldn't I live in a big house, in the middle of the town, with white steps up to the door, and men and maids to wait on me, and a carriage and pair to go driving in? 'Tis a shame, 'tis a shame, so it is, 'tis a shame!"

Well, the Fairy was disappointed, because she did hope that she would have been pleased. But she said, "Well, never you mind. When you go to bed tonight, just you turn around three times; and when you wake up in the morning, you'll see what you'll see!"

So the Old Woman went to bed that night in the little red brick house on the edge of the town, where she could see the folks going by to market, and she turned around three times, and when she woke up in the morning – she was in the grandest bed she had ever seen! It had brass knobs at the top and brass knobs at the bottom; the Old Woman had never seen a bed like it before. And when she got up and looked out of the window, it was a big house, and it was in the middle of the town, and there were white steps up to the door, and men and maids to wait on her, and a carriage and pair to go driving in.

Well, the Old Woman was pleased. But she never thought to say "Thank you" to the Fairy.

Well, the Fairy, she went East and she went West, and she went North and she went South; and one day, she came back to the town where the Old Woman was living in the big house, in the middle of the town, with white steps up to the door, and men and maids to wait on her, and a carriage and pair to go driving in. And the Fairy said to herself, "I'll just go and take a look at her. She will be pleased."

But do you know, as soon as the Fairy stood inside the Old Woman's door, she could hear the Old Woman talking to herself, and what do you think she was saying? "Oh! 'tis a shame," said the Old Woman, "'tis a shame, so it is, 'tis a shame. Look at the Queen," said the Old Woman, "sitting on a gold throne, and living in a Palace, with a gold crown on her head, and a red velvet carpet to walk on. Why shouldn't I be a Queen and sit on a gold throne and live in a Palace, with a gold crown on my head and a red velvet carpet to walk on? 'Tis a shame, so it is, 'tis a shame."

Well, the Fairy was disappointed because she did think she would have been pleased. But she said, "Well-l-l-l, never you mind. When you go to bed tonight, just you turn around three times; and when you wake up in the morning, you'll see what you'll see."

So the Old Woman went to sleep in the grand bed with the brass knobs at the top and the brass knobs at the bottom, in the big house, in the middle of the town, with white steps up to the door, and men and maids to wait on her, and a carriage and pair to go driving in. And she turned around three times, and when she woke up in the morning – she was in the grandest bed that ever was seen, with a red satin coverlet, and there was a red velvet carpet by the side of the bed, and a gold crown on a table all ready to put on when she dressed. So the Old Woman got up and dressed and put on the gold crown, and walked on the red velvet carpet, and there was a gold throne to sit on. And the Old Woman was pleased. But she never thought to say "Thank you" to the Fairy.

Well, the Fairy, she went East and she went West, and she went North and she went South; and one day, she came back to the town where the Old Woman was living in the Palace, with a gold crown on her head and a gold throne to sit on and a red velvet carpet to walk on. And the Fairy said to herself, "I'll just go and take a look at her. She will be so pleased."

So she walked right in at the Palace door, and up the red velvet stairs till she came to where the Old Woman was sitting on a gold throne with a gold crown on her head. And as soon as the Old Woman saw the Fairy, she opened her mouth and what do you think she said? "Oh! 'tis a shame," said the Old Woman, "'tis a shame, so it is, 'tis a shame. This throne is most uncomfortable, the crown is too heavy for my head, and there's a draft down the back of my neck. This is a most inconvenient house. Why can't I get a home to suit me? 'Tis a shame, 'tis a shame, so it is, 'tis a shame."

"Oh, very well," said the Fairy. "If all you want is just a house to suit you, when you go to bed tonight, just you turn around three times; and when you wake up in the morning, you'll see what you'll see," said the Fairy.

So the Old Woman went to bed that night in the Palace, in the big bed with the red satin coverlet and the red velvet carpet by the side of the bed, and the gold crown on a table all ready to put on in the morning. And she turned around three times (there was plenty of room to do it).

And when she woke up in the morning – she was BACK IN THE VINEGAR BOTTLE. And she stayed there for the rest of her life!

INHALING

Richard Hughes

Once there were two children out for a walk by themselves, when they saw an enormous policeman. He was at least six times as big as any other policeman in the world.

"I know what's happened," said the girl. "He's been inhaling too much!"

"What's inhaling?" said the boy.

"You know," said the girl, "when we have a cold, and they pour some funny-smelling stuff into a bowl of hot water and make us breathe over it. That's inhaling."

"Quite right, miss," said the policeman, in a six-times-big voice, "I have been inhaling too much: *much* too much! Would you like some of the stuff?" And he gave them a small glass pot.

"Thank you," she said. "We're rather small, you see: there'd be no harm in trying a little."

So they went home.

That night, when they were both in the bathtub, they poured some of the stuff into the hot water of the bath and immediately began to sniff it.

"This is fine!" said the little boy. "*Aren't* we growing nicely?"

And so they were; they were soon as tall as grown-up people. But the only trouble was that Nurse, who was giving them their baths, was swelling, too; and as she was big to begin with, she was now enormous.

"Put your head out of the window!" cried the boy. So the nurse did, and then, of course, she stopped smelling the stuff and stopped growing.

But the children didn't. They stood in the bathtub and got taller and taller.

"This ceiling *does* hurt my head," said the girl.

And no wonder, for they were pressed hard up against it.

All of a sudden, *crack!* went the ceiling, and pop! came their heads up into the room above! This room was their father's den, and there he sat working.

"Bless me, children!" he said, when he saw their heads coming up through the floor. "What will you do next?"

"I don't know, Father," said the girl, whose face was now above the top of his writing table.

"Bless me!" he said again. "What a funny smell!" – for the smell of the stuff began to come up through the hole in the floor.

On that, of course, he began to swell, too.

"Bless me!" he said. "Fancy starting to grow again, at my age!"

And indeed, he was soon about twice his ordinary height.

Just then, the boy's big toe got caught in the chain of the plug and pulled it up, and all the water ran away, and the magic stuff with it, and so no one grew any more.

But now they were in a great difficulty. The mother was still ordinary size, because she hadn't been there. And the nurse hadn't had time to grow very much before she put her head out of the window; but even then she was taller than the tallest soldier you ever saw. As for their father, he was twice the size he had been, and couldn't sit in his study at all comfortably, and could hardly crawl through the door. But as for the children, they were so big that, with their feet in the tub, the bathroom ceiling was only just up to their waists and their heads were just on the point of bumping the ceiling of the room above.

"What a funny family we are," they said, "with the children bigger than their father and mother!"

"However," they said, "we can't go on living in the same house, that's certain"; so they built a new house, and a very funny house it was. Their room, of course, was enormous; it reached from the basement right up to the roof, and their table was almost as high as an ordinary room, and they had washbasins as bowls. As for baths, they had to go and have cold ones in the pond; it would have taken *much* too much hot water to give them one in the house. Then came the den for their father, that was just about double size: there was a double-size table, and a double-size chair, and double-size books, and double-size papers, and double-size pipes and matches and tobacco boxes, and double-size pictures and even a double-size wastepaper basket. But the poor little mother just had an ordinary-size living-room and bedroom, and had to be very careful when she went into the children's room, that the children didn't step on her.

But as for the swollen nurse, it was much less trouble to send her away and get a new one of the ordinary size, so that's what they did!

THE MOUSE
AND THE SUN

A Canadian story

This is a story from the time long before the white men came to Canada. In those days, the animals ruled the earth. Alone on the great plains lived a little boy and his sister. Their father and mother had died when they were young. They had no uncles, no aunts, no grandmothers, no grandfathers; and so they were left to look after themselves. They lived many miles from other people. In fact, they'd never seen other people, only their parents.

The boy was very small. The girl was big and strong, and she had to find food for both of them and do all the work in the house. She took her little brother with her wherever she went, so that he came to no harm. And she made him a bow and arrows to play with.

One day – it was winter – she went out to gather wood for the fire as usual and took her little brother with her. He grew tired, and she told him to hide while she went farther on in her search for wood. "Soon," she said, "you'll see a flock of snow birds flying overhead. Fire one of your arrows, and bring a snow bird home for food."

The boy hid among the great hills of snow and watched the sky. He heard the sound of the snow birds' wings before he saw them. He put an arrow in his bow and let it fly – and another – and another. But his aim was poor, and he hit none of them. When his sister came back, bent double under her load of wood, he was ashamed to have to tell her that there was no bird for their supper. But his sister said: "Never mind. You'll get better at it. Tomorrow will be your lucky day!"

But tomorrow, when they went again searching for wood and again the little boy was left to watch for the snow birds – tomorrow didn't seem to be his lucky day. He shot and shot and shot again, but the birds flew past with a great rustle of wings. But then, at last, one snow bird fell out of the sky. He was very happy. Now he had something to show to his sister. "I shall try to kill one every day, for our supper," he said. "And you must skin them, sister, and when we have enough skins, I shall make myself a coat from them." And every day after that, he went with his sister and waited for the snow birds to fly past, and every day he shot one down and took it home. And they skinned the birds and dried the skins. Soon there were enough skins for a coat. It didn't take many – he was a very small boy.

One day – proudly wearing his coat – he asked his sister: "Are we all alone in the world? Are there *no* other people?" Well, she said, she'd heard from their mother that other people lived far away to the east, beyond the mists of the prairie: and others, the people from whom their mother came, lived far away to the west, beyond the great hills. The little boy said: "One day, I'd like to see my mother's people!" So, when next his sister was away, hunting, he put on his bird-skin coat and took his bow and arrows and set out toward the distant hills to see if he could find his mother's people.

It was springtime. The sun had melted the snow; little streams were flowing, and blades of grass had begun to show above the ground. But the earth was soft and wet, and the day was hot, and warm winds blew. The boy walked on and on, and by the time the sun was high in the sky, he was very tired. He came to a little rise in the ground and lay down behind it, out of the wind. In no time, he was fast asleep. And the sun beat down on him. It was so hot it singed his bird-skin coat, and the coat shrank and shrank until it was only a small patch on his back. And when he woke up and yawned and stretched himself, the coat burst – under his arms, across his back – it had grown so tight. He was very angry. The sun had ruined his beloved coat! He shook his fist at the sun and cried: "I'll have my revenge on you! You needn't think you're too high up there for me to get at you! Just you wait!" Without his coat, he could hardly continue his journey, so he returned home.

For weeks, he could scarcely eat. He talked about nothing but how the sun had spoiled his coat, and how he'd have his revenge. His sister tried to comfort him. Next winter, she said, when the snow birds came flying this way again, he could kill more of them, and she'd make him another coat. She'd make him two coats, or three! But he was not to be comforted.

At last, he asked his sister to make him a snare, such as you catch rabbits in – but this must be a big one, for he meant to use it to trap the sun. She made him a snare from a strip of the skin of a buffalo, but he said it wouldn't do. It

wasn't strong enough. So she cut off some of her long black hair and made a snare from that. The boy said it would do very well. And off he set, to catch the sun.

It was another long journey. But at last he came to the Great Water in the East. It was summer, and the sun rose early. The boy placed his snare where the sun would strike the land as it rose out of the sea, and then he went away and waited. Sure enough, in the morning as the sun rose burning out of the sea, it was caught in the snare and held fast. It could not rise; it was bound to the earth. "I told you!" cried the boy. "I warned you! *That's* for ruining my bird-skin coat." And he made the long journey home again.

And that day, there was no light on the earth. Everywhere it was a sort of evening, more dark than light. The animals were terrified. The birds all fled to their nests, and only the owl came out to look for food. But then, as the half-darkness went on and on, they decided they must have a great meeting to discuss what to do. So all the animals gathered together. One of the birds, a goose, that had been bold enough to fly close to the sun where it struggled in the snare, was able to tell the rest of the animals what had happened. The sun was tied to the earth! Unless they could free it, there would never again be real daylight. Someone, they decided, must go close enough to the burning sun to cut the cord that held it. It would be dangerous work, for the heat was tremendous: anyone who tried to cut the cord might well be burned to death.

They drew straws to see who should go. The task fell to the woodpecker. So the woodpecker flew to the edge of the Great Sea, where the sun was trapped, and flew closer, and closer – oh, the heat of it! – till he was close enough to peck at the snare with his beak. Alas, alas, being a strand of woman's hair, it was very strong. He picked at it and picked at it, but it would not break. At last, his head was so badly burned that he had to give up. His whole head was red from the great heat. And ever since then, the woodpecker in Canada has had a red head, where the sun singed him as the bird struggled to set it free.

Then the animals called for a volunteer to try to cut the snare. Now, at the time, the largest and strongest animal in the world was the mouse. The mouse was king of all the beasts, an enormous creature. It was his duty, he thought, to attempt that hard and dangerous task. So off he went: reaching the Great Sea in no time, so long were his legs, so fast could he run.

Once there, he attacked the snare with his teeth. But he could not bite it through. The heat was terrible. He would have run away, but kept telling himself that he *was* the biggest and strongest animal of them all: if he ran away, the smaller animals would laugh at him. So he went on, desperately using his great sharp teeth. While his back burned, and scorched, and smoked, he cut through one hair at a time. He began to melt away: the whole top of his body was burned to ash. But still he bit, and bit, and bit at that terribly strong hair. One hair after another parted. He was close to the end of his task and his whole body was melting, but now he came to the last hair of all. The hair snapped, and the sun rose free and sailed, as usual, high into the sky. It was day again. There was light again. The animals whistled, and cheeped, and grunted, and trumpeted with joy. And they made ready to welcome the mouse on his return from that brave adventure.

And here he came! Not, now, the largest animal in the world; now, almost the smallest. He was a hundred times smaller than when he set out. And his back was burned to ash. And ever since then, the mouse has been one of the smallest animals in the world; and his coat has always been the color of gray ash, from the scorching he had when he freed the sun from a snare, long ago.

KING MIDAS

A Greek legend

This story begins on a hot day, in the fields surrounding a royal palace in Greece, long ago. The sun was as golden as it's ever been, and everything seemed gold in the shine of it. The stones of the palace were really white, but they seemed bright gold. The wheat in the fields was more gold than green, and the small prince lying asleep in the wheat seemed himself to be made of gold.

As for his nurse, who came looking for him – she, too, her dress and her hair, shone as she walked. And the wheat rustled as she came through it, as if it really was made of stiff bright gold. When she caught sight of the boy, she hurried forward and stood staring down at him, for a long time. Then she gently brushed his face, picked him up, and hurried with him to the palace. She had a story to tell that the king, his father, must hear.

"Your Majesty," she said, "they were ants! First one, then another, they crawled out of the wheat and onto Prince Midas's shoulder, and so onto his face . . ."

"Well, my good woman," said the king. "If my little son *will* fall asleep in the wheat, he must expect that ants will climb over him. What do you wish me to do? Shall I order them to be executed for daring to walk on a royal face?"

"Your Majesty," cried the nurse. "Each ant carried a grain of wheat."

"Indeed!" said the king. "But ants were always thieves. Do you want me to call for my soldiers and make war on the ants for stealing my wheat?"

"But, Your Majesty," said the nurse, "as each ant came to Prince Midas's mouth, it laid its grain of wheat there and returned the way it had come. Each ant did this in turn – laid its grain of wheat on the prince's mouth and then went away. It was strange! Strange! It was as if they knew what they were doing, and meant something by it!"

"That is different," said the king. "Our ants are thieves, but they carry messages from the gods as well as any other living creature. This was a sign from the gods. My wise men will know what it means."

And indeed the wise men did know. It meant, they said, that one day Prince Midas would be wonderfully rich. It was certainly a sign from the gods. As plain as if they had spoken, the ants were saying, in taking the grains of wheat to the prince's mouth and leaving them there, that some day he would be *fabulously* rich.

And so the prince grew up with that story in his ears, the story of the sign the gods had given. His nurse talked about it often.

"Ah, my young lord," she would say, "one day, the palace will be yours, and the fields about it, and the whole kingdom."

"But that won't be all, will it?" the prince would cry. "Tell me again, nurse – what *more* shall I have?"

"Oh, my lord," the nurse would say, "how can I tell? I am only your poor nurse and never have more than a few common coins in my pocket. So how can I tell you of all the gold you shall have one day – more gold than any king has ever had who ever ruled the earth!"

"Shall I have the sun, too, nurse?" the prince would ask. "For that is the goldest thing of all!"

"My lord," the nurse would say, "how can I tell? Perhaps you will have the sun, though surely the sun belongs to the gods. I think you will have all the gold the gods can spare."

The years passed, and the prince became king in his father's place. He married a king's daughter and had a daughter of his own: and though he loved his wife, and his child, and enjoyed being king, still he was not content. When would the time come that the gods had promised, when he would be fabulously rich?

And then one day, an old man came to the palace. He was not like ordinary men. He was taller, and older, than men ever are: his eyes shone as the eyes of men never shine. He'd been found wandering and lost near the palace. King Midas knew at once that this old man came from the world of the gods. His name was Silenus, he told the king. He was the close friend of the god Bacchus. Bacchus was the god of merrymaking. And merry they'd been, the god and his old friend! So merry that Silenus had fallen asleep from all the laughing and dancing and drinking of wine. And when he woke up, he was alone and lost, there in Midas's kingdom.

So Midas gave him food, and wine, and a bed to sleep in. And for twelve days, there was laughing and dancing and drinking of wine, in honor of this visitor from the world of the gods. And on the thirteenth day, Midas himself went with Silenus to the mountain where the gods lived. It was called Olympus: and there they found the god Bacchus, who was overjoyed by the return of his friend.

"King Midas," said the god, "you have done me great

service. I had thought my old friend was lost forever. What reward will you have? I will give you whatever you wish."

And Midas thought of that old promise. "If you would give me what I wish," he cried, "what I wish for with all my heart, then . . . oh, let everything I touch turn to gold!"

Bacchus had been smiling, but now his smile vanished. "Midas," he said. "I must give it to you if it is really what you wish, for I have promised. But the gods can see further than men can see. That is a bad wish! Wish for anything but that!"

"But how can there be a better wish?" asked Midas. "Since I was a child lying under the sun, I have loved whatever is gold. I have no other wish than this. Let this be my reward."

The god sighed. "It shall be so, then," he said. "But I grant your wish with a heavy heart, King Midas. Now go and . . . enjoy it as best you can."

Enjoy it! Oh, thought Midas, as he made his way down from the mountain, how could he fail to enjoy this great gift? Now he would be the richest man on earth! He was so excited that he kept putting off the moment when he would touch something with his magic touch. Not until he had set foot in his own kingdom again, and was passing through a grove of olive trees, did he reach out a hand. It was a trembling, excited hand. And with it, he touched a hanging leaf. Strange! *Strange!* There was the leaf, soft in his hand as leaves are, and then it was heavy, it was stiff, it glittered – it was pure gold!

"Oh," cried Midas. "I can make gold with my touch! A golden leaf! A whole golden tree! Tree after tree of pure gold! Listen to the golden leaves tinkling in the breeze!" He was running wildly toward the palace, touching trees, and stones, and flowers as he went, and leaving them glittering behind him. "I can turn the very dirt into gold!" he cried. "I can turn the earth I walk on into gold!"

Now he had reached the palace. He touched its wall, as he came to it, and the rough warm stones turned smooth and bright and cold. He thought of all the things he would touch – all the common things he would turn into precious brightness and glitter. On the low branch of a tree sat a bird, a small bird, one of the palace birds so tame that it would take food from the hands of the king or the queen or their daughter. Now Midas held out his hand toward it. And the bird flew to his hand, as it always did. Warm, soft feathers, beating heart, beak open ready to sing, wings stirring. And in a second, in less than a second, it was a hard, cold, magnificent bird of solid gold! And Midas put it in his pocket and hurried into the palace.

At once, he cried for food and drink. "I've been far, and come far, and I have wonderful news!" he told the queen.

"But first let me eat and drink. I shall tell you nothing of my news until I have eaten."

In no time, a meal was ready, and the king and his queen and his daughter and all the court sat down. Everyone was longing to hear this marvelous news that Midas spoke of. Everyone was wondering why the king was so excited, so happy. The long journey had made Midas hungrier than ever before, and he reached eagerly for the food in front of him. It was good – good, warm food with a good, warm smell to it! He lifted it to his lips, and the warmth went, the smell went. His lips touched something hard and cold.

The food in his hand had turned to gold.

Suddenly, he was terrified. He dropped the golden food, and reached for the glass of wine at his side. It was cool and sweet – cool, sweet wine with a cool, sweet smell. He lifted it to his lips – and they touched something hard and cold. The glass in his hand, and the wine in the glass, had turned to gold.

The queen, and their young daughter, and all the court were staring at the king. They didn't understand what was happening.

"Don't be afraid," cried Midas. "My friends, don't be afraid! You see, this is my wonderful news. The god Bacchus has granted my dearest wish, and everything I touch turns to gold. I shall be the richest of all the men that ever lived. My daughter! I have a gift for you in my pocket – look, a bird that I touched and that straightaway turned to gold. Here it is, my dear daughter!"

And he held out the golden bird. Even as he did so, he saw the danger and cried, "Ah, *don't touch my hand!*"

But it was too late. The little girl had reached out for the glittering bird, and as her hand touched his, she froze into solid gold. Her warm flesh, her soft hair, turned to stiff, shining gold. Her dark eyes became fixed and golden. All the life left her, and she leaned cold and silent across the table with her gold hand on her father's hand.

And now there was terror in the palace.

People shrank away from the king. They dreaded that he might touch them. As for Midas, his heart had turned heavy within him when his beloved daughter changed into that dead glittering gold child. But still he could not believe that his power was a bad power. How could it be? Gold was the most precious thing in the world, surely. He could make gold with his touch. He went through the palace – the terrified, silent palace – and he touched the chairs and the tables. He touched his throne and the queen's throne, and everything turned to gold. Everywhere was the cold flash and gleam of gold! He turned glass to gold, and now you could not see through the glass. He turned cloth to gold, and now the cloth no longer stirred as it hung. He turned the palace dogs to gold, and now they no longer yawned and stretched themselves or leaped to greet the king when he came near them.

Already he had so much gold that he was twice as rich – three times as rich – now, ten times as rich – as any other king on earth. He called for the queen to come and share his joy.

"My love! My love!" he called. "Come and see how I can turn things to gold!"

But the queen had hidden herself. She was weeping for her golden daughter. She was weeping for Midas. Never again would she dare to be near the king. How could she, when one touch would turn her into a dead gold queen!

And now Midas's joy began to turn into terror. How was he to eat or drink, when what he tried to eat or drink turned at once into glittering metal? He longed to touch someone's hand, to stroke a dog and feel the living fur under his fingers. He longed to feel one thing warm, another soft, one thing rough and another smooth. He longed for the sight of wood, cloth, flesh. He longed for the poorest and most common things in the world. He longed for stones, and for the earth itself. But everywhere he went, there was the gold he had made. Everything in his silent palace was silent, gleaming gold. The very clothes he touched turned to gold. How could you wear clothes of stiff, chilly gold? In his hunger and his anger, he beat his fist against a wall, and the wall turned to gold.

"What shall I do? What shall I do?" he cried. "I'm the richest man in the world, but I'm the hungriest and the loneliest! This cursed gift the god gave me!" Then he wondered if Bacchus would take the gift back again. But *no*, he thought – *no*, he would not give it up! It was such a marvelous gift! Whatever happened, he would keep it!

And he sat on his golden throne, in his golden throne room, and tried to believe he was happy. He *must* be happy, because he was so rich!

And it was there his old nurse found him. She was not his nurse now, of course – instead, she looked after his daughter. She was a brave woman, for she was the only person in Midas's kingdom who dared come near him.

"Oh, there you are, my lord," she cried. "This won't do, you know! How could you be so silly?"

"Nurse, watch your tongue!" Midas growled.

"You should have watched your tongue yourself, my lord," said the nurse, "before you asked for this foolish gift. Now there's only one thing to do: you must go to the god and ask him to take his gift back."

"I won't," said Midas, sulkily. It was as if he was a young prince again, and she was still his nurse.

"Now, just think for a minute," she said. "How would you like a fine meal – good meat, tasty foods, and sweet things? Fruit! And wine to drink!"

"Stop!" cried Midas. "Nurse, stop!"

"How would you like to wear soft, warm cloth again, instead of those stupid, cold clothes of gold?"

"Nurse!" he cried. "Stop! I command you to say no more!"

"And how would you like to take your daughter in your arms again? How would you like to hug her? How would you like to hold the hand of your queen?"

"Nurse! Nurse!" cried the king. "No more! I will go! I will go back to the god!"

And that's what he did. He went alone, across his kingdom, to the home of the gods on the mountain, Olympus. And there he begged Bacchus to take back the gift he had given him.

"I expected you to come," said the god. "The gods do not always take back the gifts they have given. But your suffering has been great. I will remove this power from you. Listen carefully. Go from here to the great river that runs through your kingdom. Lie in the river, and let the water run over you. Then it will be the river that has the power to make gold, and you will be an ordinary man again."

And so Midas hurried back down the mountain to his kingdom. He ran through the olive grove where he had first turned things into gold. He ran past the golden trees, stiff and shining, down to the river. And he stretched himself out in the river, until the water had washed over him again and again.

Now had he lost his awful power? To climb out of the river, he must catch hold of a low branch growing on the bank. What if the branch turned to gold in his grasp? He took a deep breath and seized it. There was the good feel of wood in his hand. It didn't turn cold and stiff, as he'd been used to things turning when he touched them. He pulled himself out of the water and looked down at the river.

The little stones and the sand at the bottom glittered as if a thousand little suns were shining in the water. The power to turn what it touched to gold had passed to the river, and at the bottom of it forever, gold would be found, gold stones and gold sand.

And Midas ran back to his palace, to find that all the things he had turned to gold had become themselves again. There, waiting for him on the palace steps, was his daughter. On her warm, living hand, the golden bird was perched – but now it was a warm, living bird.

"Father," called his daughter. "Oh, father, look! The little bird wants to eat crumbs from your hand, as it always used to do! Here, father – hold it!"

Midas took the bird and felt its warm claws on his hand. The bird pecked at the crumbs in his hand, and he stroked the bird's head.

And from the bottom of his heart, he thanked the god for taking back his foolish wish.

WHY NOAH CHOSE
THE DOVE

Isaac Bashevis Singer

When the people sinned and God decided to punish them by sending the flood, all the animals gathered around Noah's ark. Noah was a righteous man, and God had told him how to save himself and his family by building an ark that would float and shelter them when the waters rose.

The animals had heard a rumor that Noah was to take with him on the ark only the best of all the living creatures. So the animals came and vied with one another, each boasting about its own virtues and whenever possible belittling the merits of others.

The lion roared: "I am the strongest of all the beasts, and I surely must be saved."

The elephant blared: "I am the largest. I have the longest trunk, the biggest ears, and the heaviest feet."

"To be big and heavy is not so important," yapped the fox. "I, the fox, am the cleverest of all."

"What about me?" brayed the donkey. "I thought I was the cleverest."

"It seems anyone can be clever," yipped the skunk. "I

smell the best of all the animals. My perfume is famous."

"All of you scramble over the earth, but I'm the only one that can climb trees," shrieked the monkey.

"Only one!" growled the bear. "What do you think I do?"

"And how about me?" chattered the squirrel indignantly.

"I belong to the tiger family," purred the cat.

"I'm a cousin of the elephant," squeaked the mouse.

"I'm just as strong as the lion," snarled the tiger. "And I have the most beautiful fur."

"My spots are more admired than your stripes," the leopard spat back.

"I am man's closest friend," yelped the dog.

"You're no friend. You're just a fawning flatterer," bayed the wolf. "I am proud. I'm a lone wolf and flatter no one."

"Baa!" blatted the sheep. "That's why you're always hungry. Give nothing, get nothing. I give man my wool, and he takes care of me."

"You give man wool, but I give him sweet honey," droned the bee. "Besides, I have venom to protect me from my enemies."

"What is your venom compared with mine?" rattled the snake. "And I am closer to Mother Earth than any of you."

"Not as close as I am," protested the earthworm, sticking its head out of the ground.

"I lay eggs," clucked the hen.

"I give milk," mooed the cow.

"I help man plow the earth," bellowed the ox.

"I carry man," neighed the horse. "And I have the largest eyes of all of you."

"You have the largest eyes, but you have only two, while I have many," the housefly buzzed right into the horse's ear.

"Compared with me, you're all midgets." The giraffe's

words came from a distance as he nibbled the leaves off the top of a tree.

"I'm almost as tall as you are," chortled the camel. "And I can travel in the desert for days without food or water."

"You two are tall, but I'm fat," snorted the hippopotamus. "And I'm pretty sure that my mouth is bigger than anybody's."

"Don't be so sure," snapped the crocodile, and yawned.

"I can speak like a human," squawked the parrot.

"You don't really speak – you just imitate," the rooster crowed. "I know only one word, 'cock-a-doodle-doo,' but it is my own."

"I see with my ears; I fly by hearing," piped the bat.

"I sing with my wing," chirped the cricket.

There were many more creatures who were eager to praise themselves. But Noah had noticed that the dove was perched alone on a branch and did not try to speak and compete with the other animals.

"Why are you silent?" Noah asked the dove. "Don't you have anything to boast about?"

"I don't think of myself as better or wiser or more attractive than the other animals," cooed the dove. "Each one of us has something the other doesn't have, given us by God who created us all."

"The dove is right," Noah said. "There is no need to boast and compete with one another. God has ordered me to take creatures of all kinds into the ark, cattle and beast, bird and insect."

The animals were overjoyed when they heard these words, and all their grudges were forgotten.

Before Noah opened the door of the ark, he said, "I love all of you, but because the dove remained modest and silent while the rest of you bragged and argued, I choose it to be my messenger."

Noah kept his word. When the rains stopped, he sent the dove to fly over the world and bring back news of how things were. At last, she returned with an olive branch in her beak, and Noah knew that the waters had receded. When the land finally became dry, Noah and his family and all the animals left the ark.

After the flood, God promised that never again would he destroy the earth because of man's sins, and that seed time and harvest, cold and heat, summer and winter, day and night would never cease.

The truth is that there are in the world more doves than there are tigers, leopards, wolves, vultures, and other ferocious beasts. The dove lives happily without fighting. It is the bird of peace.

Acknowledgments

For permission to reproduce copyright material
acknowledgment and thanks are due to the following:

Philippa Pearce for "Lion At School" (© 1971 Philippa Pearce)
from *The Lion At School and Other Stories*; Blackie and Son
Ltd. for "The Cock, the Cat, and the Scythe" by James Reeves
from *Secret Shoremakers*; Faber and Faber Ltd. for "The Fairy
Ship" by Alison Uttley from *John Barleycorn*; Jonathan Cape
Ltd. and the estate of Arthur Ransome for "The Tale of the
Silver Saucer and the Transparent Apple" from *Old Peter's
Russian Tales* by Arthur Ransome, illustrated by Faith Jaques;
Canongate Publishing Ltd. for "Beautiful Catharinella" from
Grimm's Other Tales translated by Ruth Michaelis-Jena; Faber
and Faber Ltd. for "The Autograph" by Margaret Joy from *See
You at the Match*; Puffin Books for "The Steadfast Tin Soldier"
from *Hans Andersen's Fairy Tales* retold by Naomi Lewis
(Puffin Books, 1981, copyright © Naomi Lewis, 1981);
Hodder & Stoughton Ltd. for "The Old Woman Who Lived
in a Vinegar-Bottle" by Elizabeth Clark from *More Stories and
How to Tell Them*; Chatto and Windus Ltd. for "Inhaling" by
Richard Hughes from *The Wonder Dog*; J.M. Dent and Sons
Ltd. for "Cat and Mouse" by Margaret Mahy from *The
Downhill Crocodile Whizz and Other Stories*; "Why Noah Chose
the Dove" from *Stories for Children* by Isaac Bashevis Singer.
Copyright © 1984 by Isaac Bashevis Singer. Reprinted by
permission of Farrar, Straus & Giroux, Inc.

gene perret

BUSINESS HUMOR

Jokes & How To Deliver Them

Sterling Publishing co., Inc.
New York

*"We need humor as much as we need any other kind of
sustenance in our daily lives."*
David Graves

Revision edited by Jeanette Green

Library of Congress Cataloging-in-Publication Data

Perret, Gene.
  Business humor : jokes & how to deliver them / Gene Perret.
     p.   cm.
  Rev. ed. of: Using humor for effective business speaking, © 1989.
  Includes index.
  ISBN 0-8069-9904-7 (alk. paper)
  1. Business—Humor. 2. Public speaking. I. Perret, Gene. Using
humor for effective business speaking. II. Title.
PN6231.B85P485   1998
818'.5402—dc21   98-21161

1   3   5   7   9   10   8   6   4   2

Published by Sterling Publishing Company, Inc.
387 Park Avenue South, New York, N.Y. 10016
© 1998 by Gene Perret
Portions were previously published in
Using Humor for Effective Business Speaking © 1989 by Gene Perret
Distributed in Canada by Sterling Publishing
% Canadian Manda Group, One Atlantic Avenue, Suite 105
Toronto, Ontario, Canada M6K 3E7
Distributed in Great Britain and Europe by Cassell PLC
Wellington House, 125 Strand, London WC2R 0BB, England
Distributed in Australia by Capricorn Link (Australia) Pty Ltd.
P.O. Box 6651, Baulkham Hills, Business Centre, NSW 2153, Australia
Manufactured in the United States of America
All rights reserved

Sterling ISBN 0-8069-9904-7